Retribution of Alice

By
P. T. CHAMBERS

ISBN 978-1539324447

Copyright © 2016 P.T. Chambers

All rights reserved. No parts of this publication 'Retribution for Alice' may be reproduced, stored in a retrieval system or transmitted in any form or by any means, without the prior written permission of the author, nor be otherwise circulated in any form of binding or cover other than that in which it is published and without a similar condition being imposed by the purchaser.

This book is intended for your personal enjoyment only. All characters in this publication are fictitious and any resemblance to any person living or dead is purely coincidental. Published in Ireland by Orla Kelly Publishing. Proofread by Red Pen Edits.

Dedication

For Margaret, Paula, Mark and Caroline.

Acknowledgements

A special thanks to Margaret and my immediate and extended family for their continued support and encouragement; without it this book would not have been published.

Thanks to Brian Fitzgerald for his invaluable attention to background detail.

Thanks to my Editors, Red Pen Edits, for finding and correcting my many errors and omissions.

Finally, to my publishers, Orla Kelly Self-Publishing; thanks Orla for your professionalism and support in having this book published.

About The Author

Philip Chambers, a native of Cork City, and now living in Dublin, is married and has three children and seven grandchildren.

Three years ago he decided to try his hand at writing fiction. Initially he concentrated on the highly disciplined area of short stories. Having written twenty short stories in 2014, of which five have so far been published, he decided to try writing a novel. He completed and published his first novel, 'Has Anyone Seen Alice' in November 2015. He has now also completed and published the sequel 'Retribution for Alice.'

Proverb
It's a long road that has no turning.

Retribution for Alice

Prologue

Gregg Newman was a certainty to become Mayor of Oakville City. He had everything going for him. He was young, good looking and about to become a partner in Oakville's leading law firm, Reilly Carson, Attorneys at Law. He also had the backing of a very powerful Democratic Election Committee made up of retired Judge Leo Forrest, the committee's formidable chairman Jeff Suarez, election manager and chairman of Suarez Construction Company, practising attorney Al McNally, Teddy Moran chairman of the local Farmers Bank, Doctor Jim Mackey and Gregg's boss and Senior Partner at Reilly Carson, Mark Reilly.

Gregg's only problem had been his wife Alice who didn't approve of Gregg's persistently wandering eyes and had, while under the influence of alcohol, interrupted an election meeting to berate him over his latest infidelity. Having been forcibly removed from the room by security and with the collusion of the committee, she was eventually committed to a psychiatric facility under an assumed name. A year later, Gregg filed for divorce and in an uncontested finding, was given custody of their daughter Tracey.

Three weeks before polling day Gregg was found in a confused state, sitting on the floor of his bedroom – his babysitter, Angie Lummox lying dead on his bed. He was arrested and charged with her death but was acquitted. However, he was subsequently found guilty of having sex with an underage girl and was sentenced to three years in prison.

Meanwhile, rookie TV reporter Shirley Green, with the help of Detective Eddie McGrane, discovered that Doctor Tom Mitchum at the local Minerva Clinic had come across a patient, Sarah Silver, while doing some research work in the Haven Clinic. This clinic was located two hundred miles north of Oakville. She had been committed there by a court order some years previously. While investigating that case, Doctor Mitchum had discovered ten other similar cases where patients were also committed by the courts without any review of their cases. Because there were no documents in relation to Sarah Silver, he had succeeded in having her transferred to his care at the Minerva Clinic. With patience and care he had nursed her back to health. As part of her rehabilitation and in strict secrecy, he had allowed her to use his car from time to time to visit the city. On the last occasion this happened, and just after she had returned the car to his parking space, Doctor Mitchum jumped into the car and in his rush to get home he had crashed the car on the steep driveway leading from the clinic and was killed.

After months of dogged investigations, Shirley Green had discovered that Sarah Silver was in actual fact Alice Newman. She had also discovered that Leo Forrest, Al Mc Nally and Doctor Jim Mackey were involved in her unlawful incarceration. In a blaze of publicity all three were arrested and charged with the offence.

Chapter 1

By nine a.m. every seat in the visitors' gallery of the newly built Oakville City Courthouse was occupied. Outside in the street, hundreds more, who had hoped to get a glimpse of the defendants being led into the court, were contained behind the police barriers. For the past few months the upcoming case had been the talk of the city. Not just because it was going to be the first case to be heard in the newly constructed courthouse but because it was about three 'pillars of society' that had been charged with a serious crime - a crime that would mean prison for all three if convicted. Would they be convicted and sent to prison? Would they walk free? Everyone had an opinion; some were purely political biases; some were moral or legal opinions; others were just plain old-fashioned gossip.

A petition to have the proceedings televised live had been rejected, but that did not deter the many TV stations from sending their mobile units to cover the event. However, NTTV, having local knowledge, occupied pride of place in front of the courthouse with Shirley Green, who had broken the story eight months earlier, as lead reporter for the station.

"Good morning and welcome to the NTTV Morning

Breakfast Show," began Shirley, in a confident and cheery voice. "This morning we are broadcasting live in front of the new City Courthouse where the long-awaited case of the state against three members of the Democratic Party, who have been charged with the unlawful detention of Ms Alice Newman, and who have been out on continuous bail, is about to commence."

At this stage the camera panned to the crowd in front of the courthouse where the bright summer sun lit up the red façade of the new building and the newly planted oak trees that lined the entrance to the main door. To the left of the courthouse building work was continuing on the reconstruction of the police station. The section linking the courthouse would be the first section to be completed and where the Suarez Building Construction banners could be clearly seen on the hoarding around the building site.

For over five years, ever since Ned Donnelly had been appointed Chief of Police, he had been advocating and battling to have something done with the antiquated police station. Built over sixty years ago, nothing in it was conducive to the operation of a modern police force. Now, with crime increasing in direct proportion to the expansion of Oakville City the decision to completely reconstruct the old station and attach it to the already newly built court house was underway.

In the meantime, the detective unit had been relocated to a vacant office block across the street, while the Chief's office and traffic units remained in the old building. The plan was to move the detective unit back into the newly-constructed portion of the building and then move out the other units one by one until the entire building was completed. This was estimated to take eighteen to twenty-four months – much to the frustration of Chief Donnelly. He wasn't at all happy with having his force separated. It didn't lead to the best use of time in his opinion. However, when completed, they would have a state of the art building. In the meantime, the detective and forensic units were the envy of all other units. They had at least four times the space they'd had in the old building. On the ground floor was the general reception and waiting areas and a number of small interview rooms. On the first floor they had an entire floor to themselves. Newly promoted Detective Inspector Eddie McGrane even had his own office with a conference room attached. It was he who had spearheaded the investigation that had now culminated in today's court case.

Once again the camera panned back to Shirley.

In the past eight months, twenty-nine years old Shirley Green had become a familiar face on NTTV. With her shoulder length wavy auburn-colored hair and her dazzling smile, she had become an instant hit with the viewers. It was she who had, after months of investigative journalism, discovered the missing Alice Newman in the local Minerva Psychiatric facility, which in turn led the police to uncover the plot to detain her.

"However," continued Shirley, "this isn't just about the state versus Doctor James Anthony Mackey, Mr. Leopold Maurice Forrest and Mr Aloysius Patrick McNally, in the case of the unlawful detention of Ms Alice Newman. It is about the many other unfortunate people who have been committed to institutions against their will. People who have no judicial right to have their committal reviewed - that is without the express permission of those who committed them there in the first place. And of course that permission is never going to happen - unless they are forced to do so. NTTV, together with the Oldtown Chronicle, are committed to exposing this unacceptable practice by bringing it to the highest authority in the state, the Governor's office, in order to have this situation remedied and enshrined in law" said Shirley, her eyes fixed firmly on the camera.

Then, turning to a gentleman standing beside her who was trying hard to hide his very corpulent stomach – (the result of his predilection for burgers and fries in Teddy's Diner, the local fast food outlet in Oldtown), she continued, "I have here with me Don Harding, editor of the Oldtown Chronicle. Good morning Don, and welcome to our program. Let me ask you a question," began Shirley, "in all your years as a reporter and then as an editor, did you ever come across a case like this? Tell us what your thoughts are."

As the camera focused in on Don Harding the crowds behind him craned their necks to get their faces on the news.

"Well Shirley, this is a most unusual case in so many ways. In the first instance I believe it is the first case of its kind in this state and I would go so far as to opine in the entire country. Of course it has huge implications for the campaign that we in the Oldtown Chronicle together with NTTV are spearheading to have the cases of the 'Forgotten Court, Committed Patients' reviewed independently at least every three years."

"And how is the crusade going Don?" asked Shirley, "I'm sure our viewers would be anxious to hear what, if any, progress has been made."

"Yes I'm sure they would." Harding frowned solemnly at Shirley. "But unfortunately this is a situation that will not be easily remedied. I'm afraid it involves too many parties with vested interests."

"What do you mean?" Shirley asked as she brushed

her hair back from her eyes.

"Well in each case we have a number of factors. In the first instance we have the instigator – the parent or spouse or family member who reports the case to the authorities. Then you have the medical intervention and finally you have the court system, or to put it plainly, the committal process."

"So what you are saying Don, is that in order to reverse the original committal orders, each of these factors has to be reversed. Wow – that is going to take some doing!" said Shirley, turning once more to face the camera.

"Yes, that is precisely the problem for those unfortunate enough to be in this situation," replied Harding, his face now set with a strong sense of purpose. "However, in theory, it should be easy to change the regulations for all future committals and we are hopeful that we will achieve that very soon. At the same time, we are working hard for those in the system to have a review system put in place by the Governor that will work on a case by case basis. We will not give up until we succeed."

As the camera, once again zoomed in on Shirley, she continued, "Thank you very much for sharing that with our viewers Don. And just a reminder - As part of our campaign to redress this situation, NTTV will be broadcasting a series of programs in the near future, when experts from the medical, legal and political professions will take part in an open debate on the issue." Shirley smiled – getting a plug in for the program she would soon be chairing!

Then, looking down and apparently listening to some message on her earpiece, she said, "I have just been informed on my earpiece that the defendants are already inside the courthouse. It appears that as part of the redesign of the building, the contractors have already installed a connecting corridor leading to the courthouse from the old section of the police station. The crowd who have been patiently waiting here won't be too pleased to hear that," exclaimed Shirley, looking suitably disappointed.

"In the meantime, we will continue to keep you up to date on each day's proceedings here at City Courthouse, so do stay tuned in to NTTV." Then with a flourish and a dazzling smile, she said, "This is Shirley Green for NTTV. The station that gives you the news first."

Inside the courthouse, the press gallery was crammed with reporters from almost every newspaper in the state - and some from neighboring states, all vying for elbow room. While the new courthouse had been designed to accommodate normal press numbers, no one could have foreseen a case like this one with such state-wide interest.

The courtroom was at least twice the size of the old one and the layout was far more practical. As already mentioned, it had direct access, via a secure corridor, to the old police station which was in the process of being reconstructed and which would, when finished, become part of the courthouse. It also had holding cells in the basement. This new connecting corridor meant that defendants could be brought into the courtroom in safety - without sometimes having to face the media and in some cases having to face a hostile crowd outside.

Today's case concerned three of the city's most respected and successful citizens who had been arrested and charged in connection with two offences, one, the unlawful detention, in a psychiatric facility, of Ms Alice Newman and two, the attempt to interfere with the election for City Mayor by the same act.

What made the case more interesting for the public was the fact that the three defendants were members of the Executive and Election Committees of the city's Democratic Party.

Everyone had pleaded not guilty when arrested and had been out on bail for the past number of months. Now the day had arrived when they were about to meet the full rigor of the Justice System, and the public was not going to miss a single detail of the trial.

Chapter 2

At nine twenty a.m. the prosecution team, led by Jason Miles for the DA's office, filed into their places on the right hand side of the courtroom. For the past ten years Miles had been the chief prosecutor for the DA's office with more than seventy per cent successful outcomes. Now in his late sixties he was beginning to look the worse for wear. His once well-toned body was drooping with a noticeable stomach overhang. Even though he was now almost completely bald, he still had the habit of going through the motions of brushing his hair off of his eyes with his left hand.

They were followed by the defence team who took their place at the opposite side of the room. They were led in by Bill Hemmingway, one of the state's most successful and feared defence lawyers. At six foot four inches, he emanated power and energy and positively towered over the five foot ten Miles. He was dressed in a light blue suit and matching tie and not one hair of his dyed jet black hair was out of place. As he walked to his place he turned and with a confident smile on his face bowed to the press gallery.

Sitting in front of the judge's bench were the Clerk of

the Court and the Court Stenographer. The former, stiff and formal with an air of officiousness, the latter with a look of indifference – she had seen it all before.

At nine twenty-five a.m. two court officers, dressed in tan shirts and dark brown trousers, led the three defendants into the courtroom. All three were smartly dressed and exuded confidence in spite of where they were and what they were facing. Their demeanor suggesting that this whole thing was a bit of an inconvenience and that the charges against them would be thrown out of court.

At exactly nine thirty a.m. the clerk of the court announced that the case of the state versus Mr Leopold Maurice Forrest, Mr Aloysius Patrick McNally and Doctor James Anthony Mackey was now in session – the Honorable Judge Amelia Nelson presiding.

As Judge Nelson emerged from her chambers at the left hand side of the bench, a hush fell over the room. She was a small wizened-looking woman in her late sixties with a face that resembled a walnut – over-tanned and over wrinkled, but with a reputation for her forceful and well researched findings and court decisions. She was a force not to be underestimated or tampered with.

The Court Clerk called the court to order and read out the charges. Judge Nelson asked both the prosecution and defence teams if they were ready to proceed.

"Yes, your Honor," replied Jason Miles, for the prosecution.

Jim Hemmingway, for the defence, asked that the charges be dismissed as they were, he contended, without any foundation. "I consider them to be a complete waste of the court's time and an unnecessary burden on the taxpayers of the city."

"Request denied." said the judge - not looking at him. "How do the defendants plead?"

"All three plead not guilty on both charges, your Honor," said Hemmingway.

Then turning to the prosecutor she said, "You may proceed, Mr Miles."

"Thank you, Your Honor," said Miles. "May I commence by saying that in all of my thirty-two years as a prosecutor, I have never come across a case that is, in its very essence, so despicable. It is my hope and my intention to prove beyond all possible doubt that these three defendants here before you this day, deliberately set about 'disappearing' Ms Alice Newman so that they could have their candidate elected Mayor of this city."

This caused a flurry of activity in the press gallery as this was news to them. Up to this point the case was one of unlawful detention of Alice Newman. Now it had the potential to open up a whole new charge. A political charge

- a charge of interfering with the electoral process.

Then, after shuffling a few papers on his desk, to give time for his words to sink in. He said, "Thank you, your Honor, I call our first witness, Mr Gregg Newman."

Every eye in the room turned to watch Gregg Newman take the stand. Gone was the flamboyant façade that he had presented only a few months earlier when his picture had dominated every newspaper in the run up to the election of the city's Mayor – an election he was expected to win by a landslide. That was until he was convicted on a sex charge and sentenced to three years in jail. The six months he had already spent behind bars had dramatically changed his appearance and his demeanor. His grey suit, which looked as if it was at least two sizes too big for him, now hung shapelessly on him. He had already lost over forty pounds in weight and his once well-tanned face was now a pasty grey color. His eyes had dark circles around them and bags beneath them.

Having gone through the swearing-in process and confirming Mr Newman's identity, Mr Miles said, "Mr Newman, can you tell the court, in your own words, how your ex-wife - I understand that you were divorced some years ago - ended up in a psychiatric facility?"

"Yes sir, at that time I had been selected to run for the position of Mayor and so all my energies were focused on that task. Unfortunately, at the same time my marriage was in difficulty and my wife was under a great amount of stress. This resulted in her behaving in an unsociable manner which necessitated medical intervention." said a much shaken Newman.

"Can you please elaborate on that for the court?" said Miles.

"Yes sir, unfortunately, in the months leading up to the election, and while the Party was working on my image for the electorate, my marriage was suffering, and to be honest, it was in tatters."

"I see," said Miles.

"Three weeks before the election, my wife, Alice, confronted me at an election committee meeting, making wild accusations. I was horrified and confused as to what to do. The situation was however resolved when the security guards removed her from the room and Mr Forrest told me not to worry, that he would look after everything for me – I was to concentrate on winning the election." Then pointing to the three defendants, he continued, "I later discovered that they, Mr Forrest and Mr McNally had arranged with Doctor Mackey to have her hospitalized which at the time, I thought was a very good thing for her. I did not realize until much later that they subsequently had her committed permanently, to a psychiatric facility." Newman looked mournfully at Miles.

"So you had no knowledge or input into this decision – is that so?" prompted Miles.

"Yes you are right, my marriage was effectively over at that stage so I trusted Mr Forrest to do the right thing for Alice - while I concentrated on winning the election for the Party," said Newman.

"And, if I may ask Mr Newman, over the past three years, did you ever wonder where Alice was?" asked Miles.

"Of course I did, but Mr Forrest continually told me not to worry, that she was being well looked after and that the treatment was working. He told me that in the meantime Mr McNally was arranging for a non-contested divorce so that I would be free to concentrate completely on my political career." replied Newman.

"So, having adopted you as the Party's 'Golden Boy', is it a fact that they dictated your life for you, making sure that anything that might reflect badly on you should be dealt with - in whatever manner was necessary. Is that so?" said Miles.

"Objection!" thundered Hemmingway, as he leapt to his feet. "This is pure conjecture and has no basis in fact."

"Sustained." said the judge.

"I will rephrase it." said Miles, "Did you believe that your lifestyle was being mentored by Mr Forrest and the Party?"

"Yes," said Newman. "I was constantly being advised that I was now in the public eye and that my every action was being watched. However, I was also conscious of the fact that the Party was there to protect me from adverse comment."

"So when Mr Forrest told you that they were going to take care of Alice, what did you think he meant?" asked Miles.

"I was of the belief that her mental state was not right and that the breakdown of our marriage was having a detrimental effect on her. As a result, she was drinking quite a lot. I believed that Doctor Mackey would have her treated in hospital and that she would cope better with her situation once she got her life back to normal."

"Is it your contention that all three, Mr Forrest, Mr McNally and Doctor Mackey were involved in having your ex-wife committed, under an assumed name, to a psychiatric facility?"

"It is," replied Newman.

"Thank you, I have no more questions, at this point in time." said Miles, returning to his seat.

Once Mr Miles had returned to his seat, the judge said, "Your witness, Mr Hemmingway."

Taking his time and appearing to be examining a number of sheets of paper, Mr Hemmingway slowly made his way over to Mr Newman.

"Mr Newman, I hope you can help me," said Hemmingway, spreading his hands out wide in supplication, "I seem to be a little confused after hearing your evidence – under oath! But firstly let us establish a few facts. You are the Mr Newman who was contesting the Mayoral Election last year. Is that a fact Mr Newman?"

"Yes." replied Newman.

"And having been charged with a serious sex offence isn't it true that the Party dumped you in favor of another candidate?"

"I object to the word dumped," said Newman, whose demeanor, already quite nervy, took on an even more injured appearance. "It was suggested to me that it would be better if I stepped down – which I did."

"Yes indeed you did – didn't you? Now tell me, and indeed, tell the court how you felt at having been 'dumped' by your very close friends, Mr Newman?"

"Again let me say that I was not 'dumped' as you keep on saying," replied Newman. "But to answer your question. Yes, quite naturally I felt aggrieved and upset as I felt that my private life should be separate from my public life."

"But yes, let me see," said Hemmingway as he consulted his notes, "You have just stated in your response to your very own defence team that you were constantly being advised and warned by Mr Forrest that you no longer had two separate lives. Isn't that so?"

"What I meant to say was that I didn't feel that I was guilty of what I had been charged with. Therefore, until I was acquitted or at worse convicted, I was entitled to my privacy."

"You have a most unusual way of expressing yourself, Mr Newman. Let's hope we don't spend the next few days trying to understand your convoluted answers."

As he walked away from the witness stand he half turned and, looking directly at the judge, said, "Isn't it true that you are currently a prisoner in our state prison."

"Yes."

"I want you to think carefully before answering this next question, Mr Newman. Isn't it a fact that you are now giving your version of what actually happened, in order to get back at Mr Forrest, Mr McNally and Doctor Mackey? Because you feel hard done by them? To me it certainly does seem so."

"No."

"No? Just no? Let me put it another way Mr Newman, what are your feelings towards the three defendants?"

"My feelings?" said Newman, getting animated, "I have many feelings Mr Hemmingway – I feel let down by these men whom I trusted to do the right thing for my wife. Our marriage may have been in tatters, as I said, but to commit her to a psychiatric facility without my consent or knowledge, beggar's belief. I also feel sad for my ex-wife that she is still in the clinic. And finally I feel angry at a system that perpetuates such a thing."

"Thank you Mr Newman. Very noble feelings, no doubt. But this is one of the things that has me perplexed," said Hemmingway, as he waved a form in the air. "Here we have a copy of your wife's, or should I say ex-wife's committal order…"

"Objection!" shouted Miles as he jumped to his feet, "It has been incontrovertibly proven that the signature on that committal form is not Mr Newman's signature. Mr Hemmingway has full knowledge regarding the authenticity of both signatures on that form. For the record, Doctor Mackey's signature has been authenticated, Mr Newman's has not. This is a cheap trick to cast doubt on the witness's credibility."

"Mr Hemmingway, you may get away with this kind of behavior in other courts – but not in mine. Anymore of it and I will slap a contempt of court order on you." said Judge Nelson, looking fiercely at Hemmingway. "Is that perfectly clear?"

"Apologies, your Honor," replied Hemmingway.

"I was just trying to understand how a once-renowned lawyer and candidate for the highest political position in the city, how he could not know what had indeed happened to his wife. Did he not think it strange that she had just disappeared? Furthermore, isn't it a fact that he divorced her eleven months after she 'disappeared'? I find that very strange! Very strange indeed."

"Very well, you may continue, Mr Hemmingway," said the judge, impatiently.

"Let's move on to your divorce proceedings, Mr Newman, if we may?" said Hemmingway, "I have here a copy of your divorce petition in which you state, very forcefully, I might add, that you should get custody of your daughter Tracey, on the grounds that your soon to be divorced wife Alice, was not in a position to look after her. Why? Because you had put her in a psychiatric facility! And you have the gall to tell this court that you had no knowledge of her whereabouts. Are you taking us to be complete idiots, Mr Newman?"

"Objection! I cannot see what Mr Newman's divorce proceedings have to do with the case against the three defendants!" said Miles, "This is a complete red herring."

"Mr Hemmingway?" said the judge, looking enquiringly at Mr Hemmingway.

"Your Honor, I am trying to show the court that the

credibility of the witness, a convicted felon, is not to be taken at face value against three pillars of our society. That is all I am trying to do." replied Hemmingway.

"Your Honor," interrupted Miles. "I must insist that that last statement be stricken from the record. The fact that Mr Newman was convicted of a separate crime should not be used to defame my client or cast doubts on his credibility. I am sure that some of us here in this court have been convicted of traffic offences! Should that bar us from giving evidence in criminal cases?"

"Sustained, please remove the reference 'convicted felon' from the record." said the judge.

"Mr Newman," said Hemmingway, as if nothing had happened, "can you cast any light on my dilemma? How do you explain the fact that your evidence in your divorce petition is in conflict with your evidence here in court today?" said Hemmingway.

"As I have already explained to you," replied Newman, "during that period of turmoil in my life, when on the one hand I was contesting a very tight election – the outcome of which would have changed my life completely and at the same time coping with the devastation of losing my marriage, I relied on my attorney, Mr Al McNally, to look after my best interests for me. He had told me that all I had to do was sign the papers. I trusted him completely when he told me that I had nothing to worry about. To me, that proves beyond a doubt that Mr McNally knew exactly where my ex-wife was at that time. How would he know that if he wasn't complicit in putting her there?"

"Very clever Mr Newman. However, I put it to you that he knew it because you instructed him to carry out your despicable wishes. He knew it because he was, as your attorney, carrying out your instructions... No more questions." replied Hemmingway as he made his way back to his desk.

"Thank you Mr Hemmingway." said Judge Nelson. "The court will recess until two thirty p.m."

Chapter 3

At two thirty precisely the Court Clerk intoned "All rise. The court is now in session," as Judge Amelia Nelson once again took her seat on the bench.

"You may proceed Mr Miles." Judge Nelson nodded to the prosecution's desk. "Please call your next witness."

"I now call our next witness, Doctor Quintin Moody."

All eyes turned to see who he was - but for a number of minutes nobody appeared. While waiting for the witness to enter the courtroom Judge Nelson tapped her fingers impatiently on the bench. Eventually the witness did appear, walking slowly down the aisle with the aid of a very ornate walking stick. He was immaculately dressed, but in a somewhat outdated style. Above his well-tanned face was a full head of snow white hair. He was wearing an off-white suit with a red waistcoat. He looked like a character actor from a Tennessee Williams play.

Having carefully positioned himself in the witness seat and having been sworn in, he turned and smiled at the judge and said, "Good afternoon, your Honor."

Judge Nelson was not amused and let him know it with one of her withering looks. Turning to the prosecutor she said, "Proceed with your witness Mr Miles."

"Doctor Moody, for the record, can you tell the court how long you have been a medical doctor?" began Mr Miles.

"Yes indeed, it is true; I have been a doctor for many many years - in fact more years than I care to remember. You see," he said warming to the question, "I qualified precisely forty-eight years ago and immediately began as an intern in our local general hospital where I stayed for three years before getting a post as a junior doctor...."

"That's fine Doctor." said Miles cutting him off in full flight. "We don't need a full history. Now can you tell us when you retired from practice?"

"Well, in reality I didn't retire fully until last year, you see, having been all my working life in various hospitals around the state, I took up private practice on a semi-retirement basis when I moved up to Wayward Creek about eight years ago," replied the doctor.

"I see. Now tell the court, when you were living in Wayward Creek did you, as part of your 'semi-retirement' practice, attend many patients in the nearby Haven Clinic?" asked Miles.

"Yes I did." replied the doctor. "In my first few years there I attended a few patients on a casual basis. Then I was given responsibility for one particular patient. This I did for a number of years."

"And do you recall that patient's name?"

"Yes, I have checked my notes and the patient's name was Sarah Silver."

"Your Honor," said Miles. "I would like to record into evidence, as Exhibit A, the affidavit from the District Attorney confirming that the 'Sarah Silver' in question is in fact Alice Newman."

"Duly recorded," replied the judge.

"Can you please tell the court the circumstances under which you became Sarah Silver's doctor even though you were not in any way employed by the Haven Clinic?" Miles resumed.

"It was most unusual indeed." replied Moody. "One day, I think it was a Monday, if I am not mistaken; I was visited by a gentleman whom I had never met before. He introduced himself as Doctor Mackey from Oldtown."

"Is that gentleman present here in this courtroom?" Miles asked.

"Yes," replied the Moody.

"Can you point him out to the court?'

"That is he," said the doctor, pointing to Doctor Mackey.

"Let the court note that the witness has identified Doctor James Anthony Mackey as the person in question," stated Miles.

"Will you now tell the court what the purpose of that visit was?"

"Doctor Mackey proposed that I take responsibility for a patient of his who had been transferred from Oldtown to the Haven Clinic. He told me that she was a dangerous woman who needed constant sedation as she was subject to hallucinations and thought that she was a well-known politician's wife whereas in fact she was just a law clerk."

"Did he prescribe the medication and dosage to you?" Miles asked.

"Yes, he was very specific in his instructions," he replied with a smile.

"Your Honor, if it pleases the court I wish to enter Doctor Mackey's notes as 'Exhibit B'." said Miles. "You will see from these notes that for two years Doctor Moody, under instructions from Doctor Mackey, administered daily sedation to a patient who was registered in the Haven Clinic as a Ms Sarah Silver. We now know this patient to be Ms Alice Newman. No more questions, your Honor."

"Your witness, Mr Hemmingway," said the judge.

"Thank you, your Honor. Now Doctor Moody," began Hemmingway as he slowly made his way across to the witness box in a threatening manner. "For forty years you practiced in, let me see, seven different hospitals that is according to your record, a copy of which I have here.

Is that correct?"

"Yes, that would be correct. I'm sure you are aware of the importance of moving," began Moody.

"I'm not interested in the fact that you moved around, Doctor Moody," interrupted Hemmingway, "but I am very interested in the reason why. During that whole period, you never progressed to a senior position in any one of those seven hospitals. I find that strange, don't you?"

"I never sought glory, Mr Hemmingway." responded Moody, self-righteously. "Perhaps you do. Maybe that is why you ask that question. I was always content to look after my patient's wellbeing and that does not need titles or positions of honor."

"If that is your mission in life, why then did you leave so many hospitals during those forty years to, as you put it, to practice in the small town of Wayward on a semi-retirement basis? Had you some connection with that town, Doctor Moody, or maybe you had another more personal reason for leaving the hospital and moving north?"

"Your Honor, I must protest at this line of questioning," interrupted Miles. "Where is it leading? Doctor Moody's career path has nothing to do with the case in hand."

"Mr Hemmingway, what exactly is the point you are trying make?" asked the judge.

"Your Honor, if you will permit me to continue with

this line of questioning I hope to establish the reliability, or otherwise, of this witness." responded Hemmingway.

"Very well, you may proceed but don't try my patience, Mr Hemmingway," replied the judge.

"Doctor Moody, is it a fact that, in the week prior to you moving to Wayward Creek you had to sell your home and furniture and your car, in order to pay off your substantial debts?" said Hemmingway as he stood directly in front of the witness box.

"Yes, Mr Hemmingway, that is true; like so many thousands of other folk I did overextend my credit during the boom years. But then, when it was opportune, I wanted to start a new life, debt free. Is that a crime Mr Hemmingway? If it is then I can assure you there are many criminals present in this court," snorted Moody, getting his dander up and a laugh from the gallery.

"Touché, Doctor Moody. However, did you not think it strange that a doctor, who was unknown to you, should seek you out and ask you to look after a patient for him?" Hemmingway responded. "What kind of inducement did he make to you to undertake such a program, a program that you have just said was unusual, to put it mildly?"

"Yes indeed I was surprised, but then it was always the case where doctors helped each other out in difficult circumstances," replied Moody. "Of course we did agree on a financial arrangement. I'm sure you don't think I did it pro bono, do you? I doubt if you help out your colleagues for nothing."

Another laugh from the gallery, warming to the little old man.

"Let me be a little blunter," said Hemmingway, his voice rising, "When you decided to retire from your position in the state general hospital, were you in financial difficulties?"

"Objection!" shouted Miles, "Doctor Moody has already addressed this innuendo. The witness has given incontestable proof that he acted on instructions from the defendant, Doctor Mackey. This line of questioning has no relevance on these proceedings other than an attempt to sully the character of our witness."

"Court recessed," said the judge, banging her gavel on the bench. "I want to see both counsellors in my chambers immediately."

With that the judge left the bench and both counsellors followed her into her chambers while the defendants and the majority of those in the room took the opportunity to stand up and exercise their cramped limbs having sat quietly without moving for fear of drawing down the judge's ire on them.

When they were in the judge's chamber, Judge

Nelson, turning to Hemmingway said, "Mr Hemmingway, please explain to me the point you are trying to make and what the relevance of that point, if there is one, has in relation to the case?"

"Your Honor, I believe that Doctor Moody was compromised by the fact that he was in financial difficulties and that as a result, his testimony is flawed," said Hemmingway.

"And what proof do you have that the doctor was in financial difficulties?" responded the judge.

"I don't have hard evidence," replied Hemmingway, "but I have unconfirmed information that he has or had a gambling problem, I am trying to get the information from him by way of my questioning."

"Mr Hemmingway, my court is not an interrogation room. If you have evidence – bring it to me. Otherwise this is the end of your line of questioning. Is that understood?"

"Yes your Honor." replied Hemmingway sheepishly.

When the court had reconvened, Hemmingway continued with his cross-examination.

"Now Doctor, let us return to what you allege were the instructions you received from Doctor Mackey. Do you really expect the court to believe that, as stated in your deposition testimony, that you fully remember and understood what these instructions were?"

"With all due respect sir I have no problem in that regard," replied Moody.

"Let me remind you that you are under oath and after all you are an octogenarian who has retired many years ago and no doubt you have not kept up to date with modern medicine. I put it to you that while you may think you remember," said Hemmingway with a confident smile while opening his hands again in a gesture of appeal as he faced the judge. "In fact you do not remember clearly. You have been briefed by the prosecution to peddle this version of the truth. It is pure fiction!"

"I may look senile to you sir," said Moody as he sat forward in his seat, his eyes blazing, "and I may be a little older than you are sir, but I was always taught in my profession to be absolutely sure of my facts before I used the scalpel. Do you really believe that I would take a verbal instruction to administer such an unusual sedation from anyone without getting a proper written prescription and instruction?"

It was as if he had been hit by a ten-ton truck – Hemmingway just stopped and stared at him. "Are you now telling the court, that you actually had written instructions? You said nothing about that in your deposition document!" Hemmingway appeared to have lost all composure.

"I don't know about your profession sir," replied

Moody, with a smile, "but in my profession we insist on proper administrative procedures being in place before we proceed with the simplest of practices. Of course I was given a full and detailed instruction and prescription from Doctor Mackey, as I have stated in my sworn deposition." replied Moody, with a smile. "And if that is not enough for you, I have it here in my pocket if you wish to view it. Luckily for me I was able to find it yesterday."

The blood drained from Hemmingway's face. You could hear a pin drop in the silence that followed.

"May I make a request that the court recess until tomorrow morning your Honor? I need to consult with my clients," requested a very flustered Hemmingway.

"Have you any objections Mr Miles?" asked the judge.

"No your Honor," replied Miles, with a satisfied grin.

"The court will resume at nine thirty a.m. tomorrow." said the judge.

With that Hemmingway escorted the three defendants to an interview office beside the judge's chambers.

Chapter 4

When the three defendants and Hemmingway's two assistants were seated around the table, Hemmingway refusing to sit, was pacing up and down the room like a caged animal, before finally addressing Doctor Mackey.

"What the hell kind of game do you think you are playing at? Did you not think it important to tell me that you had given Moody written instructions? What chance have you given me? You left me twisting in the wind, that's what you have done. You might as well have signed a complete confession. Now we have a serious problem, you are directly linked to the offence. Gentlemen, this is not looking good for any of you. Doctor Moody may look like a push-over but as you can see, he is up for it and has the judge eating out of his hands. Every effort to discredit him has, so far, backfired. But above all, his notes are critical to the case. Of course I will contest their authenticity and whether or not they are allowed to stand."

"So far, only Mackey is implicated in this," said Forrest. "Do you think they have much to implicate Al and myself?"

"They would not have charged all three of you if they did not feel that they had reasonable proof. However, now that you brought it up, I would like all three of you to consider an option."

"What do you mean?" asked Mackey.

"What I mean is that at present all three of you are charged with the offences and if one of you is proven guilty, all three of you 'go down' in one way or another."

"So what are you suggesting?" asked McNally.

"I'm not suggesting anything," replied Hemmingway. "I'm just saying that over the next few hours, and before each of you are called as witnesses, each one of you should 'think outside the box' and guide me in trying to get the best deal for all of you. Is that clear? Now when we go back tomorrow, I will be calling each of you as a witness – so remember, win or lose your private lives and actions and the Party's dirty linen, will be splashed on every TV and newspaper by that evening. I am now going to leave you so that you can discuss your options."

As soon as he had left the room, both McNally and Forrest rounded on Mackey: "Why the hell did you do that, you stupid fool?" commenced Forrest, "Has your brain gone to sleep?"

"Hold on a second," responded Mackey, standing and facing Forrest, his face reddening. "It was your idea to contact Moody. He was your contact! Do you think he would have agreed to do the job without proper documentation?"

"Look, fighting among ourselves isn't going to do us any good," said McNally, "I think Hemmingway was pointing us in a definite way forward."

"What do you mean?" asked Forrest.

"Jim those notes of yours are damning, that is unless he can challenge their authenticity," replied McNally. "There are no two ways about it. If we are convicted, we will probably get three years each. In addition, this case will last for four or five days and each of us and the Party will be dragged through the mud. Party Headquarters have made that very clear to me that they are not impressed. Apart from that, our careers and reputation will be in tatters."

"I see where you are going," said Mackey, his voice rising and beads of perspiration forming on his forehead, "You want me to take the rap, is that it? But no way am I going to take the blame and spend three years in the slammer for something that you organized. Go find another sucker."

"Easy on Jim," interjected Forrest. "Let's not slam the door on a possible solution by adopting an attitude of 'if one gets jail we should all get jail.' If you ended up in jail it would not have a serious effect on your career – after all you are retired from practice, your wife is dead and you live alone. For Al and me it would be a very different story. It would have a very serious effect on our careers and on the Party. As it stands right now there is a distinct possibility that we might all end up in jail, so let's think about it and talk to Hemmingway this evening."

Chapter 5

Later that afternoon Hemmingway and the three defendants met in his plush offices downtown to reviewing the day's proceedings and to plan strategy for the following day, Hemmingway began, "Gentlemen, first of all tell me how do you think this morning's proceedings went?"

"Not so good," said Forrest. "You seemed to have had a problem trying to shake either witness."

"How do you think I could do that when we offered them their case on a plate? That disclosure of Jim's instructions really means 'Game, Set and Match' unless we can counteract it somehow. However, I must admit that I am not very hopeful of being able to do that now. Maybe it is time to think of damage limitations, and see what options we have."

"We were discussing that at the recess break after you left us." said Forrest. "But we didn't come to any definite conclusion. However, we did get the feeling that you were leading us in the direction of looking for some kind of a deal. Were we right?"

"Well, look at it this way - worst case scenario - let's suppose you are all found guilty on both counts, what kind of sentence would you get? While it is hard to say with certainty, I estimate that you would get three years each with one year suspended."

"Christ, I don't think I would survive even one year behind bars, as you know I have a dicky heart, not to mention my other ailments." said Al.

"Just for argument's sake," said Leo. "If one of us was to change our plea to guilty and assume full responsibility, exonerating the other two, do you think they would offer some kind of deal to the one. After all it would save them a lot of time and resources. Of course, let me hasten to add, I'm not saying which of us that could be."

"It's a lot to ask any one of you to make that call," said Hemmingway, "but if you did agree among yourselves, you would have to fully support the person making that sacrifice while he is serving his sentence. On the other hand, I would have to make the best deal possible with the DA: Two years with the second one suspended. Who knows then what our new 'Democratic' Mayor Erin Sullivan might be able to swing for us. But firstly we would need to agree a plan and then we must presume that the DA would be open to a deal."

"When would you need to know our decision?" asked Jim.

"To have any chance of a reasonable deal and to avoid further damaging publicity, we would need to be meeting with Miles no later than seven or eight o'clock tonight."

"Christ, that doesn't give us much time." replied Al.

"Look, I'll contact Miles and sound him out – just to see if he is willing to deal. That way, if he is open to dealing, he will make himself available. Also it gives him time to let his boss know that we are thinking along that line. Call me when you have made your decision and good luck."

For the next hour the three friends debated and argued, sometimes hotly, over which of them was the most culpable, and which of them had the least to lose, dragging the debate around in circles. While all agreed that they were all complicit in the decision to commit her, each one tried to make a case as to why one of the other two should take the rap. Eventually, in desperation, Leo said,"From the evidence given today, all of it can be contested by showing that Gregg has had an issue with us. The court may not believe our version but at least it is there to be worked on. However, the one piece of evidence that can't be contradicted is your note Jim. In my opinion, that damns you specifically."

"I knew you would get around to that," shouted Jim. "Blame Jim has been the name of the game ever since we started this 'debate.' There never was another alternative in your mind, was there?"

"In reality Jim, I suppose there wasn't once those notes were accepted by the court, there could be only one outcome," said Al.

"Look Jim," said Leo, "I know it's not easy and who knows but the DA may not entertain Hemmingway's proposal, but assuming he can do a deal, which hopefully will give a lesser sentence than all three of us would get, you would be getting a better deal overall, isn't that the truth? And rest assured we will look after you."

"Damn Moody!" said Jim, "why the hell did he have to keep those friggin' notes? To look at him you would bet your bottom dollar that he would have mislaid them within an hour of getting them. Damn damn damn!"

"One other thing," said Leo. "I'm sure the Party would make a substantial donation to your homecoming when you get out."

Finally, a very crestfallen Jim said, "OK, it looks like we all go to jail or I go on my own. Phone Hemmingway and see what kind of deal he can make."

Chapter 6

As soon as Hemmingway got the call from Forrest, he called Miles on his cell phone.

"Hi Miles, Bill here. I wonder would you be available for a short 'off the record' conversation? I could be at your office in ten."

"Sure, why not. Make it thirty; I have someone with me right now."

"Thanks, I'm on my way."

Twenty minutes later when he arrived at the DA's office, he was ushered into a functional meeting room – a table and four chairs; nothing like the style of the rooms in his own building. Fifteen minutes later Miles arrived together with Mary Donnelly, the DA.

"I hope you don't mind me including our DA in this conversation. I have a feeling that sooner rather than later she will be involved."

"No problem. As a matter of fact, it is good thinking." Hemmingway said, as he shook hands with the DA.

"Anyone like coffee before we start?" asked Miles.

"No thanks," said Hemmingway, "I appreciate you seeing me at such short notice. The reason I wanted to see you rather than just call you is the sensitivity of what I am about to say."

"We fully appreciate that," replied Miles.

"Ok. So hypothetically, and off the record, what would your reaction be if one of the three was to change his plea to guilty, taking sole and total responsibility for the crime and exonerating the other two?"

"I would wonder why we should consider such a suggestion – it being hypothetical of course," replied the DA.

"Well personally I could see a number of reasons to consider it," said Hemmingway. "This case has the potential to do untold damage to the democracy of how this city works. By the time the case has dragged on into next week, both political parties will be pitted against each other by the media that will exaggerate and embellish every argument and every response from both the prosecution and the defence. Matters that had best remain just rumor will be presented as fact – until proven otherwise. But like mud thrown at a wall, some of it will stick. Finally, I believe that while I may not be able to get all acquitted, I will get some."

"You always had a way with words Bill," said Miles. "So what exactly are you proposing?"

"I have asked my clients to agree among themselves the best way forward. I have suggested to them that, whether intentionally or otherwise, an offence has been committed, so there must be retribution – I accept that. However, I would suggest that the decision to have Ms Newman removed from the room in the first instance was to have her receive medical help. Unfortunately, that medical intervention progressed from admission to detention and finally to committal." replied Hemmingway.

"And what decision did your clients come to?" asked the DA.

"I don't know. I left them to come to an amicable agreement and told them that, in the meantime, I would get a feeling for what kind of response we would get from you," said Hemmingway. "If you offer a reasonable deal, I will sell it to them. Have no fear of that."

"Ok, give us an hour to think about it and I will call you with our decision." said the DA.

Thirty minutes later, Hemmingway got a call from Miles.

"Hi Bill, I think we have something to offer – but not on the phone. Can you get back here to us as soon as possible?"

"Yeah, I'm just around the corner grabbing a sandwich – it's been a long day, I don't know about you but I needed some sustenance to keep going. I should be with you in fifteen to twenty minutes."

Fifteen minutes later he arrived at the office and after

the usual pleasantries, Miles said, "Ok here is the deal and it's non-negotiable. Doctor Mackey changes his plea to guilty and signs a written confession to the charge of unlawfully committing Ms Alice Newman, against her will and under an assumed name (Sarah Silver) to the Haven psychiatric facility in Wayward Creek. Secondly that he arranged with Doctor Moody to ensure her detention there by administering, on a daily basis, enough sedation to take away her ability to function in a normal manner. The purpose of all of this was to remove an obstacle that could possibly hinder Gregg Newman from winning the Mayoral Election."

"I think that that is reasonable," said Hemmingway, "but what about the other two defendants? Will you file a nolle prosequi for them both?"

"Yes, that is agreed," said the DA. "However, regarding the sentence, we have no say in that and as you know Nelson is her own woman and she is just settling into this case and might be a bit humpy at having it being pulled prematurely."

"Ok, I'll draw up the confession and when you approve it I will get the doctor to sign it. That may not be so easy without some kind of inducement by way of a lenient sentence." said Hemmingway.

"As I said, sentencing is totally in the hands of Nelson.

We will however be pleading for a reduction in the three-year mandatory sentence, due to the admission of guilt," said Miles.

The following morning Doctor James Mackey was sentenced to three years' imprisonment, without remission, by a very disgruntled Judge Amelia Nelson.

Chapter 7

"Hi Shirley, feel like getting together for something to eat later?" said Eddie when he eventually managed to track her down. Detective Inspector Eddie McGrane and Shirley Green had been seeing each other regularly over the past six months. Maria, Eddie's police partner, told everyone that she was the first to see Eddie fall for the 'TV girl,' as she called her. Almost two years previously, thirty-six-year-old Eddie's marriage had ended in divorce and he was determined not to try it again, that was until he met Shirley. She was different - or so he told all of his buddies who were joshing him.

"We had a long session with the kids this evening, trying to prepare them for the quarter final on Saturday. Now I'm starving and don't feel like going home hungry." In his spare time Eddie coached the Oakville Junior soccer team. Before he had 'done in' his knee he had been a keen player himself.

"You must be telegraphic Eddie. I was just thinking the same thing. Do you think Mario's would fit us in?"

"There you go again Shirley! I was think more of a KFC takeaway and you translate that into a table at Mario's Place. I knew I shouldn't have brought you there on our first date AND I think you mean telepathic and not telegraphic. You are too young to remember telegrams!"

"Now Eddie McGrane, I have a feeling that you have already booked that table – you know the one in the corner by the bay-window. Give me time to take off my makeup and I will be ready in fifteen."

"Shirley Green, you must be the only woman in the world that takes off her makeup when going out on a date. We are still dating, aren't we? And yes the table is booked. How am I ever going to be able to pull the wool over your eyes?"

"Don't even try, mister!"

Fifteen minutes later – Eddie was a stickler for time. If he said 7:15 pm, he meant 7:15pm. He was ringing the bell to her apartment.

Ten minutes later, having kissed and hugged as if they hadn't seen each other for months on end they were in Eddie's car heading for the restaurant. Eddie said, with a twinkle in his eye, "You were great on the show this morning and you didn't look too bad either…"

"One more remark like that Eddie McGrane and I swear I won't marry you – even if you begged!"

"I can see that this is going to be a really exciting night. By the way, who said anything about getting married? I certainly didn't. It must have been your poor mother hoping against hope that someone would take you off her hands!"

Before Shirley could counter, they had arrived at Mario's.

The drive had taken them along the north shore of the lake, past the yacht club and back into Mario's restaurant which was situated right on the western side of the lake shore. It was Eddie and Shirley's favorite eating place. The steaks were second to none and of course, Eddie was well known there; the owner Giovani was, like Eddie, a coach for the Oakville Junior team. As a result, the service they always enjoyed was special. One of the things that Shirley liked about Mario's was the way everyone seemed to know each other. A number of the customers turned out to be buddies of Eddie and the chit-chat and banter between them was always nonstop. From the first time Eddie brought her there she had felt completely comfortable. She liked Eddie's friends. She also liked the steaks there. And she loved Eddie.

"You know Eddie," said Shirley when she had devoured a twelve-ounce steak with fries and a mixed salad; which she did regularly without appearing to put one ounce on her size eight frame. "I think that when, and I am not promising anything, that when we get married we should have our evening meal here at least every other evening."

"And I suppose those evenings would be the ones when you would be scheduled to do the cooking. Nice try Miss, I think that before we go any further we had better employ a marriage counsellor right now. I am beginning to smell trouble with a capital T."

Later on when they eventually broke free from all the friends and banter, they headed back to Shirley's apartment. Both had early starts in the morning; Shirley was scheduled to be outside the courthouse by 8:15 a.m. with her TV makeup on her face while Eddie was due to meet up with the Chief at the station at eight a.m., before reporting to the courthouse for day two of the trial. Eddie wasn't completely at ease bringing Shirley back to his own place, even though Shirley and he had repainted it completely. It still held memories of his short marriage, which had ended in divorce roughly two years previously. Most week nights they stayed in their own apartments and stayed in Shirley's at weekends. Now, like a couple who were completely at home in their respective skins, they were seated at either end of the couch with Shirley's feet resting on Eddie's lap while they watched the Late Show on TV and talked about the future.

"Do you, Mr Detective, know that Confucius said that to have no regrets is the beginning of happiness? Do you have any regrets?" asked Shirley.

"Before I answer that, my love, I want to know who the hell this guy Confucius is and where I can find him – to sort him out."

"Oh God, I despair of you. You are a complete Philistine. Did you ever go to school – no, I take that back! You obviously didn't. Sorting you out is going to be a lot harder than I thought and I'm beginning to doubt my ability to do something about it."

"Ah don't give up just yet! It's worth everything just to see how your mind works. I now have a better understanding of why Butch, your boss, the poor man is on sedatives!"

If Eddie was looking for a reaction, he got it by way of Shirley's foot in the stomach.

"I think he used to say that for every action there is always a reaction," said Eddie as he grabbed her foot and started to tickle it until she screamed. "And for your information Miss, you are probably referring to the Confucius who was born more than two centuries ago, did you know that? He was a great guy for philosophical sayings; most of them unproven rubbish!"

"Is there no getting the better of you Eddie McGrane? If I didn't know you better, I would say that what you have just done was a very – at least you thought so – clever ploy to get out of answering my question and I nearly fell for it. Be warned, I am on to your tricks mister Police Man!"

"OK, regrets? Yeah I have a few but to be honest, the one that jumps out at me right now is that I didn't meet you a few years earlier – then I wouldn't be carrying some of the scars that I have. Now let's change the subject and tell me more about you and Butch and NTTV!" replied a somewhat embarrassed Eddie.

"Oh Eddie, you can be so romantic. And, for the record, that is my regret also. If only I had met you earlier, I would probably have had you sorted out by now!"

"Ok, enough of that," said Eddie, not feeling comfortable with the direction the conversation was going. "Tell me what's new at NTTV?"

"Well, as you know, Butch and Don worked together in Oldtown as reporters for the Chronical. That was before Butch moved up to Oakville to work in NTTV, eventually becoming Station Boss, and Don took over as editor at the Chronical. They both share the same set of ideals with regards fighting for the underdog."

"But I thought you mentioned that Don had no interest in anything to do with Oakville?"

"Yeah, that's what he told me the first time I met him in Oldtown, but old habits die hard, especially for reporters. So when I suggested to him that a campaign to rectify the position where people could be committed to a psychiatric facility without that committal automatically being reviewed every three years – he couldn't wait to get involved."

"So, what's the plan?"

"Well, so far we have just had a preliminary meeting to adopt an overall strategy as to how the Chronical and NTTV would work together effectively. To my way of thinking, that is too slow. But they feel that because of the type of people who may not want the hornet's nest upturned, it would be better to go softly-softly and initially just create an awareness of the situation. Then the pressure will be seen to come from the public. That is why the TV program we are planning is going to be so important."

"Sounds like a good plan to me," said Eddie.

"Well it all depends on getting the right type of people on the panel. That's my immediate problem."

"In what way?"

"I think it important to have a balance of political, medical and social input on the show. We must get the politicians involved. While the medical and social input will set the scene, it is the politicians who will ultimately call the shots."

"Looks to me you have a busy week ahead of you, now let me see if I can distract you from it for a while." said Eddie, putting his arms around her.

Chapter 8

"The sooner they complete my new office the better!" exclaimed the Chief as the sixth person, Doctor Bill Power from the Minerva Clinic eventually arrived and squeezed into a corner of the Chief's small office. "Much as I like you all, I'm getting fed up of breathing in the air that you expel – it can't be good for the mental process! When our DA, Mary Donnelly requested this meeting I thought it easier to hold it here as it would be more time consuming if we all had to travel to her office. Now I'm not too sure it was a good decision."

Detective Inspector Eddie McGrane and his partner, Maria Diego, the District Attorney Mary Donnelly and the Chief's assistant, were already seated around the room.

"I know you are all very much aware of the delicate position we have here regarding the unsolved murder of Angie Lummox," began the DA. "We know that Gregg Newman was acquitted on that charge so he can't be charged again. The next big question we have to ask is: was Alice Newman involved in the death of Angie Lummox? The items we discovered hidden in her room at the Minerva Clinic would appear to point in that direction. The second question then would be, if so, was she insane at the time or not?"

"That's the sixty-four-thousand-dollar question." said the Chief.

"Yes, it is. Our immediate problem is that we can't interview her until we unravel the circumstances surrounding what we now know to be her unlawful incarceration. So in my opinion the process should be, firstly to establish whether or not she was sane or insane while she was committed to the psychiatric facility and then to establish if she is now a sane person in the eyes of the law." said the DA.

"Yes indeed, you have hit the nail on the head," replied the Chief. "Ever since Alice was discovered in the Minerva Clinic six months ago we have been closely examining her situation. Perhaps if we look at your final question first, I'm sure Doctor Bill Power, by conducting the normal set of tests for that sort of thing along with his colleagues, can readily answer that for us. Is that so, Doctor?" said the DA, looking at Doctor Power.

"Yes indeed, you are quite right in that regard. We, in our profession have re-introduced a standard procedure for clearly identifying the sanity or otherwise of such patients. It is, if I may say so, as watertight as we can possibly have it." Doctor Power said while referring to his notes and stroking his full beard - a beard that seemed somewhat out of place on someone as young as the doctor. "Since taking over from the late Doctor Mitchum I have been quietly monitoring Alice's recuperation but have not, as agreed with you," continued the doctor, turning to Chief Brennan, "done any of these tests on her."

"So, in your opinion Doctor, when do you feel it would be appropriate to start these tests?" asked the DA.

"Well," replied Doctor Power, "in spite of what Alice has gone through over the past three years she would appear to be responding very well to the program that the clinic has devised for her; indeed, it is just the continuation of the program that the late Doctor Mitchum devised before his death. I would however mention a word of caution; she is, in my opinion a very scared and angry woman who needs to be handled with care."

"At what stage do you think we will be in a position to question her about the items we found in her room at the clinic, Doctor?" asked Eddie, eager to get around to interviewing her.

"Oh I think we are a long way from that, Detective. We have to take it stage by stage. Firstly, we have to build up her confidence in the system. Remember that for three years the system not only let her down but actively tried to destroy her as a person. It is only thanks to the late Doctor Mitchum that she is in as good a condition as she is now.

As I mentioned to you on the phone last Tuesday, we have applied to the court to have a lawyer appointed to represent Alice with immediate effect. They have appointed a Mr Tim Bradshaw. However, we haven't met him yet."

"Another issue that will have to be resolved and, this will be up to the courts, is the divorce that her husband Gregg got while she was incarcerated." said the DA.

"That's going to be a very interesting court decision." said Maria, "I presume the current divorce findings will have to be reversed or annulled or whatever and then a fresh divorce proceeded with. That could probably mean that Alice would get custody of their daughter Tracey. Now that's going to mean a lot of counselling for all concerned. I wonder how Gregg will handle it when he gets out of jail."

Turning to the DA, the Chief said, "I presume we are within our rights to retain the items we found in her room and that the results of our examination of them for fingerprints and DNA residues will still be valid."

"Yes, that search and the finding of those items, the ski mask, latex gloves and the computer print-out of the power steering and brake systems of cars, was carried out under a legal search warrant at that precise point in time. You may take it that anything you found may be used at a later time. Of course that is not to say that a good defence lawyer wouldn't try to have it discounted."

"Ok Eddie," said the Chief, turning to face him, "while we are waiting to interview Ms Newman, check in with Lennie in forensics and verify that every item we have has been thoroughly checked for prints and DNA and is not in any way tainted or contaminated."

"Ok Chief. Just one point I want cleared up. Since the court has convicted Doctor Mackey in relation to the unlawful incarceration of Ms Newman, does that not mean that she is now free to come and go from the clinic as she pleases?"

"Yes and no," replied the DA. "Yes, since the court has ruled that she was falsely incarcerated, technically she should be free to go. However, the answer is no, not until she has been assessed as to her current mental state. Just remember what she had been subjected to for three years without anyone to listen or to help her."

Turning to the Chief, the DA said, "I think it might be a good idea for you to arrange a meeting with that lawyer who has been appointed to represent her – what's his name?"

"Tim Bradshaw," interjected Eddie.

"Oh yes, and then for both yourself and Doctor Power to meet up with him and be seen to work together to get to the bottom of this unfortunate affair. Let me know how you get on," replied the DA.

Chapter 9

In a profession where style, brashness and exuberant confidence seemed to be accepted as a must, Tim Bradshaw stood out like a sore thumb. Over six-foot-tall with a mop of blond hair falling down on his rimless glasses his skeletal thin body, was like a broom-stick on which his shiny new suit hung without shape. He looked more like an absentminded professor than a lawyer. Those who met him for the first time would invariably completely underestimate his ability, which was understandable as his whole demeanor was one of self-effacement.

Two years previously he had graduated summa-cum-laude at a college in the nearby state and had been spotted and recruited by the small local Oakville law firm of Menzies and Steen. Its partners, Sean Menzies and Nicky Steen, both of whose parents had come from Europe and had settled in Oakville setting up a small law firm specializing mainly in personal litigation cases. Never ones to rock the boat, they set about building up their law firm slowly brick by brick. They were always content to take the business that the more established and politically-inclined law firms weren't interested in. In this way they made a tidy living and were never seen as a threat to the bigger firms who were even happy to pass on clients from time to time.

When Tim Bradshaw was appointed to represent Alice Newman it was commonly seen to be a case of 'appoint someone who has not a vested interest in what Alice Newman says or does.' In other words, get a safe pair of hands. He can't do any damage. None of the bigger and more established law firms wanted to get involved in what was seen to be a potential political minefield.

Up until his appointment, Bradshaw had dealt mainly with insurance and personal accident cases where he was beginning to achieve a reputation for his uncanny knack of blind-siding his opposing lawyers.

Now as he walked into the office of Mary Donnelly, the District Attorney, he looked boyish and shy and awkward.

"Good morning, Mr Bradshaw," said Mary as she welcomed him into her plush office and introduced him to Doctor Power. "I appreciate you taking the time to meet up with us. I think it very important that we work together in helping your client, Alice Newman, get her life sorted out, don't you think?"

"Yes indeed Ms Donnelly," began Tim, in a very quiet but forceful voice, "I'm sure you will agree that the state has been very negligent in how it allowed such a travesty of justice to be perpetrated against my client."

"Oh, I think that is a very broad statement to make, particularly at this point in time when, as well you know, the state has already identified those responsible and has indeed punished them," replied the DA.

"If I may add to what the DA has said," interrupted Doctor Power, "One must always have regard for and knowledge of practices and procedures that were in vogue at the time. Hindsight is always perfect. In this particular case however, it would appear to me that even those flawed procedures were ignored."

"Perhaps," retorted Bradshaw, holding Power's gaze until he looked away, "on the other hand, it might be a case of the state finding a convenient scapegoat."

"Look Mr Bradshaw," replied the DA, "maybe we should start all over again. I don't think that where we are going is going to get us anywhere fast. Let me put my position clearly on the table and then perhaps you can do the same. How about that?"

"Very well, let's see where you are coming from," said Bradshaw with the hint of a smile.

"In my opinion," said the DA, "we have to look at Alice Newman the victim who was incarcerated in a psychiatric facility – against her will. Then we have to look at Alice Newman the possible suspect in the murder of Angie

RETRIBUTION FOR ALICE

Lummox who was found dead in the home of Alice's then ex-husband, Mr Gregg Newman. Now, regarding the first point, there is no denying that damage – serious damage – has been done to her and the court has recognized that and identified Doctor Jim Mackey as the person responsible for it. The court also exonerated her husband, Gregg Newman, Mr Leo Forrest and Mr Al McNally of any wrong-doing in that regard."

"That is true," interjected Bradshaw, "but sometimes the law is an ass."

"Regarding the second point," continued the DA, ignoring his remark, "your client admitted that on a number of occasions, while dressed in black and wearing a ski mask, she entered Gregg Newman's house, without his knowledge or permission."

"Yes the court did clear the people you mentioned but perhaps certain other people were pulling the strings in the background. While I agree with what you have outlined I do believe that this whole travesty of justice has its genesis in the political scene and I would hope to get to the bottom of it. Until we get to the bottom of this, Alice Newman, my client, will never get justice."

"So where do you propose to commence?" asked DA Donnelly.

"At the moment my client is penniless, homeless and

still committed to the Minerva Clinic. The first two issues are as a result of her 'divorce' and so my first task will be to have that resolved as a matter of priority."

"But a divorce can't be overturned." interrupted the DA.

"That remains to be seen and I am sure you will agree, will depend on what the court decides. I have already petitioned the Family Court to review the case and am awaiting word back from it."

"Excellent, that would seem to be a very good way to start," she said. "We all agree that your client needs justice and we fully sympathize with her. You can rest assured that our office will give you every support we can in achieving that justice for her. It should be a very interesting legal debate which I believe will, in many ways, criss-cross our efforts to establish Alice's mental state before and during her incarceration. Hopefully we will be able to assist each other in this area." The DA looked hopefully at Bradshaw.

"Thank you." Bradshaw nodded formally. "However, I must take exception to your inference that my client was or could possibly be in some way involved in the murder of Angie Lummox. To even suggest that is preposterous. How in God's name could my client have been in any way involved in what, from what I recall hearing, was a clever and complicated murder? Was it a case of police incompetence in the case against her husband that he was cleared of the charge? Or were there other leads that were ignored due to jumping to the easy solution and being over-confident with the case? These and all other aspects of the case will need to be looked into at a later date. Naturally I will want full disclosure of all aspects of the interview the police had with my client and the interview notes. I particularly need confirmation that her rights were not in any way violated during the interview. Furthermore, regarding compensation for her lost years, I will also be filing documents in that regard at a later date."

At this point both the DA and Doctor Power began to realize that the fumbling, apologetic and hesitant man sitting across from them was not going to be an easy 'push-over.' He was going to be a formidable opponent. He was about to open up a can of worms and they needed to tread warily. They needed an excuse for a recess to make sure they were united in their plan going forward.

"Well, none of us want to make life any more difficult for Alice if we can help it." said the DA. "However we are still looking at an unsolved murder and we will investigate it in our usual thorough manner. We are currently waiting to get the go-ahead to interview her. Isn't that right doctor?" she said, turning to Doctor Power.

"In my opinion I think it very important not to rush

the process." said Doctor Power. "Alice needs to adjust to all that has happened to her in the past few weeks before she would be up to the rigors of an interview. I believe that will take another few weeks at least. As soon as that day comes we will advise the police."

"You can rest assured that we will not commence any interview without advising you beforehand." said the DA.

"Thank you." said Bradshaw.

"Can I suggest we take a ten-minute break? Just to stretch our legs?" suggested the DA.

"Good idea," said Doctor Power.

When they reconvened the meeting the DA said, "I want to mention another delicate issue in connection with the divorce; have you given any thought to the plight of Alice's daughter, Tracey?"

"Yes of course we have," replied Bradshaw. "She is central to all of this, but until we sort out the divorce, my thinking is that she is better off staying with her aunt where she has a normal family environment. It must be devastating for her to realize that her father is in jail and her mother is in a psychiatric facility; not a very healthy background for anyone, least of all a fragile ten-year-old girl."

"Certainly not a good background for anybody but hopefully we will be able to sort out the technicalities and then the rehabilitation can fully get underway." said the DA.

Just then there was a knock on the door and a young lady put her head around the door and said, "Just reminding you that your next appointment is waiting for you."

With that the meeting came to an abrupt ending with all promising that swift progress would be made and agreeing that the DA would convene another meeting the following week.

Chapter 10

As Oakville City continued to expand so did the workload of the police department. Eddie McGrane now had an additional two detectives assigned to his unit. But even that didn't seem to lessen the workload. Now that summer had arrived with unusually high temperatures – especially for early July – activities around the lake increased the need for proactive policing. Eddie could never remember having to deal with so many breaches of the peace taking place at this time of the year. It was suggested that perhaps it was the heat – the result of climate change.

So far this year he'd had to deal with three attempted murders and at least twenty cases of violent assault on the person. Also he had an exceptional increase in aggravated burglaries to investigate. This was compounded by the fact that for the summer months, the population of Oakville increased by up to thirty per cent, mainly holiday makers availing of the excellent water sport activities that were available all along the lake shore. This in turn offered opportunities to hundreds of students seeking summer employment which at times brought them into conflict with migrant workers from other parts of the state.

He needed a vacation. So did Shirley.

"I really need a break from here," began Eddie, as he watched Shirley putting together one of her special salads while he perspired over the barbeque.

"Good thinking," said Shirley, "where will we go?"

"My mind must be going on me," answered Eddie, "I don't recall saying the word we, did I? Whoops!" he said as he caught the onion Shirley had fired at him. "Reflexes are not so bad, are they honey?"

"You will need to keep them that way if you are going to continue with that kind of smartass talk, mister."

"Well, I'm due three weeks leave but the Chief doesn't like us taking any more than two at a time. He feels that if you are away for three weeks, things get out of control. On the other hand, he actually told me to take time out. He thinks I work too hard! Would you believe that? How are you fixed? You must be due some time off at this stage, now that you have Butch around your little finger."

"The day that I have my boss around any of my fingers – look up and you will see pigs flying!"

"Seriously, I reckon I can have sufficient loose ends tied up to be able to get away in two or three weeks' time. That would be just before the schools close and the families head for the beaches."

"Did you say beaches?"

"Yeah, I think we need a sea breeze to keep us cool, don't you?"

"Wow, tell me more!" said Shirley coming over and putting her arms around him as he flipped two more burgers. "What exactly do you have in mind? Tell me quickly and first thing in the morning I'll be knocking on Butch's door, watching him drool when I tell him that we are heading for the beach!"

"You'd not better ask him for the time off before you make him drool? It could end up with the two of you drooling!" said Eddie with a smile.

"Right as usual mister. God I hate it when you do that! Anyway I'm scheduled to go up to Charlestown College to see if I can get more definite information on the late Doctor Mitchum's research into the whole area of committals to psychiatric facilities. That needs to be done before I have any hope of getting the time off that I need."

"Ok, you check on your availability and I'll check my diary and see if we can find a one or, even better, a two-week slot to get away."

Chapter 11

The following morning as Eddie was reviewing his case load with his team he got a call from the Chief to drop across to his office. Having negotiated his way through the building's hoarding and scaffolding he made it to the Chief's office where he found him with perspiration showing through his shirt. He had discarded his jacket which was unusual for him. In short he looked hot and bothered.

"Hi Eddie, this place is like a sauna. They tell me it is not worth their time trying to do something with the air-conditioning system as my new 'all singing and dancing' office will be ready before they would have had it fixed. But they don't have to work in these conditions!"

"Would you not think of moving across to our unit? Especially since I have decided to take your advice and take a vacation? Shirley and I have decided to head to the beach for two weeks, starting three weeks from Friday. You could have my office all to yourself and the air-conditioning is great."

"Friday three weeks? But that's only a few weeks away! I know I said to take a break but Eddie what am I going to do when you are gone?"

"Well for starters boss, you're not going to contact me. My cell phone will have developed a chronic malfunction, due to excessive exposure to the sea breeze. However, you can depend on Maria. As my partner, she is fully up to date on all of my files and she has the support of one hell of a great squad. So don't worry."

"Don't worry? It's easy for you to say that. But ok, if you have to take a vacation – go and enjoy it and come back with a few solutions to our backlog of cases." The Chief consulted his notes. "Now what I called you over for was to fill you in on the meeting the DA and Doctor Power had with Tim Bradshaw. It appears that the wimpiest looking Tim Bradshaw is not as wimpiest as he looks. He is, according to Mary, going to be a handful. One of the issues he brought up was the interview yourself and Maria had with his client, Alice. The one you had when we got the warrant to search her room at the clinic. He wants full disclosure of the interview notes and confirmation that her rights were not compromised."

"That should be no problem Chief," said Eddie. "The interview was fully recorded as usual and if my memory serves me right, when she said she would not answer any more questions without a lawyer being present, we stopped."

"Good, but I'm not one hundred per cent sure how we

stand with the items we discovered in her wardrobe. Did we have the right to remove them? Mary is of the opinion that we had. No doubt but time and Tim Bradshaw will tell."

"Well, when we find black ski-masks and latex gloves and documents on car power steering and micro-security cameras I think we were within our rights to have them checked. So I would be inclined to go with Mary's assessment," said Eddie. "Apart from photographing them in situ and checking them for fingerprints, we have just stored them in a safe environment."

"I know that until we get to interview Alice we can't proceed with the case. However, now that we have some idea of what Tim Bradshaw is planning, we had better be ready for every eventuality. Have a word with Lennie in forensics and make sure we have our findings as clear as crystal."

On leaving the building Eddie heaved a sigh of relief when he got back to his fully air-conditioned office. In the short time that he had spent across with the Chief, his shirt had now stuck to his back with perspiration. Eddie had the greatest of sympathy for the Chief and all other units who were still trying to work in the old building, in what some people referred to as a building site. Luckily enough, forensics was just down the corridor. He didn't even have to phone Lennie for an appointment. He just arrived at Lennie's office.

"Well, have you just had a sauna or something?" said Lennie when he saw the condition Eddie was in. "My guess is that you were over with the Chief. I can't believe our luck in getting these fantastic offices just cos he decided to stay in the old building while the rebuilding was going on. And we got this palace!"

"Don't count your chickens before they are hatched," said Eddie. "He might just be in the process of changing his mind right now. He must have lost at least fourteen pounds' weight through perspiration this week. I can't see him putting up with it for another month. He may decide to swap with us."

"Oh God no…don't even say that as a joke! So, what's on your mind? What does the Chief want from us now?"

"One thing I will say about you Lennie," continued Eddie, "is that you don't beat about the bush! It's straight out, what does he want? Yeah, apparently the state has appointed a young cub lawyer as free legal aid to Alice Newman and the DA had a meeting with him yesterday. Apparently he is no push-over according to her. So, to quote the Chief, 'check out with Lennie and make sure all the t's are crossed and i's dotted'."

"What t's and what i's is he talking about?" asked Lennie.

"You remember when we searched Alice's room in the clinic," replied Eddie, "and found the black ski mask and literature on surveillance equipment and the working of car braking systems? Well he obviously just wants to be sure we didn't overstep the mark in any way."

"Oh those t's and i's, well that's easy, isn't it? We did everything according to the book – no shortcuts."

"Yeah, that's true, but while we checked for fingerprints, we had nothing to compare them with as we were not in a position to get Alice's prints. Also, as far as I recall, we found two different sets of prints on some of the items and again they didn't turn up on any of our data bases. Oh, and one other thing, we weren't in a position to check from whose laptop/printer the printouts came from. At the time everything seemed to point to Gregg being as guilty as hell. Maybe we left a few t's uncrossed!" Eddie waited for all of this to sink in.

"Damn! Right now we can't go anywhere near Alice but maybe if we came up with some way to get all the staff fingerprinted we might get lucky. Remember Doctor Mitchum is dead, so he is off the list."

"True," said Eddie. "But remember we and his wife Beth have so many items belonging to him. Surely we can extract his prints from some of his personal items." said Eddie.

"Yeah, I think that would work." Said Lennie, "I feel it very important that we have him on file as he played a very central role in the whole affair. Now, regarding the staff, it isn't public knowledge that we found anything in Alice's room. So if we were to put it out that we were investigating the theft of Doctor Mitchum's watch and needed to clear all of the staff by fingerprinting them, no one should object as in reality no watch was stolen."

"Hold it Lennie, I think that would get us in a whole bucket of trouble – I don't think that would be legal but I will run it past the Chief and see what he says. Nice try Lennie - thinking outside the box as usual! But remember, Tim Bradshaw is now watching us."

"Ok." Lennie conceded, "I'll call out to his widow and get the doctor's prints and compare them with what we have got on the items. You go and see how we can fingerprint the rest of the staff and let me know when we can move it on."

Getting up and pacing the room and eventually addressing Lennie, Eddie said "Maybe we are just pussyfooting around the problem and tying ourselves in knots." Eddie scratched his head. "We are after all investigating a murder and as such there is no reason why we can't print the staff if we think that is justified - just as long as we don't go near Alice. Isn't that right Lennie?"

"Sure, but I feel we were negligent in not doing that at the time. It now may look that like we are in some way covering our tracks. And that may weaken our case eventually."

"I take your point but we are as they say, where we are. We need to get a conclusion on this. Most likely we will just have eliminated ten to twenty from our investigation. I think we don't have a choice. Let's do it."

"It's your call Eddie, you set up the operation and we will do it immediately and quietly."

"What are we waiting for? Now is as good a time as any to get cracking. We can fill the Chief in later, if necessary," said Eddie as he extracted his cell phone. "I should have the clinic number here."

Getting straight through to Matron Sue Smyth at the clinic he explained to her that the police were clearing up a few lose issues in relation to the death of Doctor Mitchum. He then explained that it would be necessary to have the entire staff of the clinic fingerprinted. Sensing her concern, he assured her that this would be done very discreetly and that it was the only way of making sure that there would not be a shred of doubt over any of her staff. Reluctantly she agreed and promised to get back to him with a suitable time as soon as possible.

"Let me know when you get the go-ahead and I will

set up a team to get it done within an hour. If my memory serves me right, the full staff number is twenty-five. I assume we are talking about the medical and administrative staff only?" said Lennie.

"Right, as usual," smiled Eddie as he headed out the door.

Chapter 12

When Shirley had convinced her boss Butch to initiate a campaign for inmates of psychiatric facilities who were there under court orders to have their cases reviewed by an independent tribunal, she had no idea of the minefield she was about to enter.

In her naivety she thought that all she had to do was contact all of the psychiatric facilities in the state and ask each of them to advise her of the number of such inmates.

However, when she tried that approach, the result she got was a blanket statement from all claiming patient confidentiality and in a few cases the threat of legal proceedings if she persisted with her investigation.

She then tried her luck with the legal system and wrote to all courthouses in the state looking for access to their records for the same purpose. The response was clear. Stay away. Such cases were held in camera and as such, guarantee confidentiality.

Now, in the comfort of her apartment and having just finished washing the dishes after cooking Eddie's favorite Italian meal – at least he always said it was his favorite one! She was now about to commence working on her laptop, preparing for her TV program. Walking over to Eddie, who was slouched on the couch in front of the TV, she pleaded. "Eddie, I need help," as she fluttered her eyelashes at him.

"I agree; you do need help. Have you tried talking to a shrink?" replied Eddie, as he focused on the ball game he was watching on TV.

"Very funny bunny," replied Shirley as she moved in front of the TV. "You know how much I depend on your superior knowledge and wisdom; don't you honey? Please help me and I won't ask you to marry me again today."

"How can I resist such an offer? What's up Doctor?"

Having told him of the rebuttals she had so far received and how far out on a limb she had crawled in order to convince Butch that she knew what she was doing, she now felt stymied.

"Well it is obvious that the wagons are being circled." said Eddie, his eyes still focused on the TV. "Those who committed family members to the clinics certainly don't want anyone interfering with the system. What you need is a whistle-blower who would be willing to spill the beans from within, but that's not an easy ask."

"Whistle-blower! But how would I get one of them?"

"Not an easy task," said Eddie as he shifted his gaze to Shirley, giving her his full attention for the first time. "Perhaps a few TV programs pulling at the heart strings might ferret out some one. Or maybe a few articles in the Oldtown Chronical. On the other hand, this whole exposure came to light when the late Doctor Mitchum inadvertently came across it when he was acting as consultant to a number of clinics, so that information must still be available somewhere. You recall when we visited Charleston College we were told that he had actually sent a proposal to the Governor - a proposal that was ignored, from what I remember. All you need do is find that. Now would you mind moving your butt from in front of the TV please?" said Eddie as he craned his neck to see what was happening on the TV.

"You are so endearing Eddie. Just one small thing; where should I start looking for the late doctor's submission? Any suggestions?"

"How about getting in touch with that absentminded professor we talked to the day we visited Wayward Creek? Remember he actually got back to us with some information on the doctor's submission. At the time I recall you saying that you'd bet he is a hoarder. Now is the time to find out if you are right or not."

"God bless your memory Eddie McGrane. You really are my savior. Pardon me while I try and find my notes on that encounter. If I remember rightly, we met two doddery professors on that day!"

Just as the ball game was entering its nail-biting

end, Shirley came bursting back into the room waving a notebook and crying, "I found it! I found it!"

"Well thank God for that! Now just let me watch the last two minutes of the game and you'll have my total and undying attention – as always."

One thing you could say about Shirley, was that she was thorough in whatever she did and always kept detailed notes. Butch had instilled that culture in all of his journalists. Shirley now came under that description: a maker and keeper of accurate notes. He maintained that once you brought an event out into the open you never knew when you could be challenged. Now, as soon as the game ended and Eddie had turned off the TV she triumphantly opened her notebook for Eddie to see.

"There you are," she gloated, as she read out her notes:

Visited Charleston College with Detective Eddie McGrane.

Met the College Administrator, Mr Ike Bolton.

That was followed by a synopsis of her conversation with the administrator regarding the missing Alice Newman, who had graduated from the college some years previously.

She then found the notes she was looking for: Introduced to the retired Dean of the Psychiatry Faculty,

Professor Steven Hurst who remembered well the late Doctor Tom Mitchum. That was followed with very detailed notes on how he remembered Doctor Mitchum and in particular, his concern for patients who had been committed by the courts.

"That's it. I'm off to Charlestown in the morning. Care to come with me? If only for old-time's sake?" asked Shirley in her little-girl voice.

"Sorry honey but tomorrow is a no-no." replied Eddie. "Now if you were to wait until Saturday, I would love to go with you and meet up with the doddering professor. I bet he won't even remember meeting us and telling us so much."

"Great, Saturday it is! But first let me contact Ike Bolton, the guy who set up the original meeting, and see if he can arrange for the professor to meet us on Saturday. Who knows but old Hurst could now be singing with the angels for all we know."

Having been assured by Bolton that the professor was still alive and available to meet them on Saturday, she set about preparing for both the journey and the meeting.

Saturday morning, they woke to another cloudless sky and brilliant sunshine. The heatwave that had started two weeks earlier was due to continue unabated. In order to avoid the midday heat Eddie suggested that they leave as early as possible. For Shirley, remembering the difficulty they had in finding a place to get a snack on their last visit north she had decided that having a picnic was the way to go. That meant that she didn't intend taking any chances. Having checked that the ice-box was packed with everything but the kitchen sink and especially the fresh rolls prepared for their lunch, she was satisfied that they were ready to go.

At seven thirty a.m. they headed off and arrived at the college at nine thirty a.m. Their appointment with Ike Bolton, the College Administrator was for ten a.m. That gave them time to have a look around the campus and to review their strategy for the meeting.

Once again, as they walked around the campus they were amazed at the wide range of sporting facilities that were available to the students. "I wish I had those facilities when I was a student." commented Eddie.

"Well I must confess I was never the sporting type, music and readings were my loves." replied Shirley.

Realizing how far they had walked they had to make a mad dash back to the administration building.

"Good to see you both once again and please accept my congratulations on your success in locating Alice Newman," said Ike Bolton as he ushered them into a pleasantly cool room overlooking the broad tree-lined avenue that led to the main administrative building. "I read all about it in the local papers. It got great coverage here."

"Thank you," said Shirley. "Indeed it was our chat with you and the fact that you put us in contact with Professor Steven Hurst, that opened up the case for us. Now we are hoping that Professor Hurst may be able to help us again."

"Well, as I mentioned to you on the phone, poor old Steven is getting more and more forgetful every day. Hopefully today will be one of his good days."

Just then Professor Hurst entered the room; both Shirley and Steven were taken aback at how much his appearance had deteriorated. His head, with its unruly mop of snow white hair was stooped, with his chin almost resting on his chest. He was now walking with the aid of a walking stick. However, whenever he looked up at them from over his glasses, his blue eyes still sparkled with life.

"Well if it isn't Tom Mitchum's friends. What a pleasant surprise," said Hurst when he saw the visitors. "And how is dear Tom keeping? I keep meaning to contact him. We were very close colleagues you know." As he shuffled towards the nearest seat and sat down heavily.

"Yes indeed, we do remember you telling us how close you were. That is why we called to see you today." said Shirley. "You may recall telling us of Tom's interest in a certain number of patients he had come across who were committed by the courts …"

"Yes, indeed I do!" interrupted Hurst. "Those poor patients were just locked up and the key thrown away. But Tom wasn't having any of it, was he? No, he wrote letter after letter to the Governor – for all the good that did. He might as well as have been whistling in the wind."

"When we were talking to you on our previous visit you mentioned that he had approached you for advice on the matter." Shirley continued. "Do you by any chance, have any notes or dated correspondence in relation to his appeal to the Governor?" asked Shirley. "The Governor's office denies having had any such approach from Mitchum."

"That's ridiculous! Of course he appealed to the Governor. However, that was a long time ago but let me check my records and if I find anything I will get back to either Tom or yourselves. They are not going to get away with that lie… no siree." said Hurst, jabbing his finger at Shirley.

Turning to Bolton Shirley asked, "If Tom Mitchum was in correspondence with the Governor's office on a regular basis, would there be any record on the college computer of that correspondence?"

"If he had used the college system, yes, there should be, but I would hazard a guess that he would have used his own laptop. However, I have been proven wrong before, so let me check it out for you. It may however take some time, but leave it with me."

Satisfied that they now had two possible avenues being explored, they thanked both gentlemen and bid them a good day.

On the journey back they discussed the possibility of Hurst even remembering them let alone finding some records of three or four years ago. Shirley was of the opinion that Hurst was a hoarder and that she believed that his once great memory, which he had proven to them on their previous visit, was still active if just temporally asleep. Eddie was of the opinion 'once you lost it, it was gone,' end of story. For God's sake, he thought that Mitchum was still alive. How is that for memory – dead or alive?

Having agreed to disagree on that issue they then discussed their future plans. Yes, they would get married and yes they both wanted at least three kids. Then Shirley curled up in the seat and with a smile on her face, slept for the remainder of the journey.

The following Monday, Steven Hurst rang back to say that he had located his old diaries. Unfortunately, his notes were not very precise. To be honest they were a mess. However, one such note referred to a date on which one submission was made and more importantly he had the name of the person to whom the submission was sent.

Next day Ike Bolton called to say that he had found one letter on the college main computer. It was just a two-line letter but it did give a date and it did refer to previous substantial correspondence. Enough for Shirley to quote during the upcoming TV debate.

Chapter 13

It was the beginning of August when the petition for the examination of the divorce, which had been granted in the marriage of Gregg Newman and Alice Newman, was eventually heard in camera at the Family Court. At the initial hearing of the petition with Judge Ellen Breen presiding, neither Gregg Newman nor Alice Newman was present. Gregg Newman was represented by Joe Breslin, who had successfully defended him the previous year on the charge of murdering Angie Lummox. It wasn't apparent why Al McNally wasn't representing him again. Tim Bradshaw represented Alice Newman.

Turning to Bradshaw the judge said, "Mr Bradshaw, you have petitioned the court to overturn the uncontested divorce which was granted to the appellant, Gregg Newman, almost three years ago. Is that so?" she asked.

"Yes your Honor." replied Bradshaw as he knocked the file from his desk while attempting to stand up. "My apologies, your Honor," he muttered as he fumbled to pick up the pages that had scattered around him.

"Very well, Mr Bradshaw. Please proceed with your arguments in favor of your petition. I assume you do have a rational basis for taking up the court's time?"

"Thank you, your Honor. Yes, indeed I do. But let me clarify my position if I may, I am not here to ask for an annulment or anything like it. In fact, I am here to prove that there never was a divorce. You see, your Honor, I contend that the court erred in granting a divorce decree to Gregg Newman and that in fact, the court decree thus granted has absolutely no validity in law."

"Your Honor, this is ridiculous!" interjected Breslin, "I admire this young man's enthusiasm. I do believe it is his first case," he threw in for effect. "Is he seriously asking us to believe that our legal system is so bereft of integrity that it would grant such a grave dissolution of a marriage without being absolutely sure of all of the facts surrounding the marriage? And to add insult to injury he has the audacity to cast aspersions on the character of one of our finest and most able lawyers, Mr Al McNally who acted for Mr Newman in his divorce petition," thundered Breslin.

"Thank you for your interruption, Mr Breslin," said the judge, looking anything but grateful. "I do hope it won't happen again. You will be given ample time to put your arguments to the court. Now, please allow counsel for Ms Newman to outline his case."

"Thank you," continued Bradshaw, having regained his momentum. "Your Honor, I agree with the learned and much older Mr Breslin. It does seem unbelievable that the obvious flaws in that case have not been seen or if they have, that they were ignored. Maybe it is just that I am not long out of college that I still remember the basic tenets of law. Correct me if I am wrong, your Honor," said Bradshaw, looking up at the judge from under his mop of hair, "but I was taught that for a contract to be legally binding, one of the basic conditions was that both parties were to be of sound mind and fully understood what they were entering into and were doing so freely."

"That may be so in theory," replied Breslin, before the judge could respond. "The facts are however that Alice Newman signed the necessary papers which were witnessed by none other than their family attorney Mr Al McNally, one of the most senior respected and competent lawyers in the city. I will restate the facts for you Mr Bradshaw: a divorce, once granted cannot be annulled. It's as simple as that."

"Yes, Mr Breslin," said Bradshaw, again getting to his feet and fumbling with his notes. "But again, to my mind, and this is where it gets very interesting." He said as he appeared to be looking for some particularly interesting note on his desk. "You see, before this case I was advised of Mr McNally's prowess, but obviously that doesn't do justice to his amazing attributes. Not only is he a learned and well regarded lawyer but he obviously has other hidden talents…"

"Please, your Honor put a stop to this rambling or we will be here all day!" interjected Breslin.

"Yes, Mr Bradshaw, please come to the point," said the judge.

"I assume you are all very much aware that earlier this year the pedigree of the aforementioned Mr Al McNally was being questioned in court in connection with Alice Newman's illegal incarceration."

"Objection!" roared Breslin. "I object to this slur on Mr McNally's good name. He was cleared of all charges in relation to that case!"

"Sustained." said the judge. "Please refrain from any further such comments, Mr Bradshaw."

"Apologies your Honor, but while Mr McNally was cleared of any wrong-doing, by his own admission he was involved in the events that led to Ms Newman being committed to the clinic."

"And what, if anything has that to do with this petition?" asked Breslin.

"I am just examining the integrity of Mr McNally. You see it now appears that he has the power of bi-location. Let me explain, your Honor." said Bradshaw as the judge looked at him as if he had completely lost the plot. "If you look at the divorce papers you will see that both Gregg Newman and Alice Newman signed the papers two years ago on the fifteenth of March at eleven thirty a.m. and both signatures were witnessed by the aforementioned Mr Al McNally. Isn't that correct?" said Bradshaw, looking from Breslin to the judge and back again to Breslin.

"Yes, that is stating the obvious," responded Breslin, testily.

"Ah now, that is where it gets really interesting," said Bradshaw, with a twinkle in his eyes. "You see, on that day, our friend, the magician, was also in court in Oldtown, acting on behalf of the Farmers Bank in a case against a certain Mrs Willow who had defaulted on her mortgage. The records of that case show that the case went on for the full morning. Now while this was happening in Oldtown, Alice Newman, registered as Sarah Silver, was ensconced over two hundred miles north in the Haven Clinic. Sedated up to her eyes, if we are to believe what we were told. Do you find that strange? I certainly do."

"There is obviously an error in the date. Nothing sinister at all," replied a much shaken Breslin.

"That may be the case, and then again it may not," muttered Bradshaw, again shuffling papers on his desk. "The other thing that puzzles me is the integrity of our legal system; a matter which our learned friend, Mr Breslin has just lauded. You see your Honor, for the Family Court to grant the divorce it had to be sure that both parties were compos mentis. Isn't that so?" asked Bradshaw.

"Yes of course, that is basic law," replied the judge testily.

"Ah yes. But less than a year previously, our very same legal system, albeit a separate court, had declared Alice Newman insane and saw fit to incarcerate her in a psychiatric clinic, where she is still confined to this very day, having been declared legally insane. Do you see my problem your Honor?"

What had started out as a very routine case for Judge Breen was rapidly becoming a nightmare. She needed advice.

"Thank you Mr Bradshaw. I do indeed see where you might have problems. In the light of your submission, I will seek further advice. In the meantime, this case is adjourned and will be reconvened again on Friday morning next. Good day gentlemen." said the judge as she hurriedly left her bench.

For once in his life, Joe Breslin was speechless. He had ended up with egg all over his face. He never saw it coming. In fact, he had been so confident that he would have the application for dismissal wrapped up within an hour that he had arranged to play golf at noon with none other than Al McNally and two of his friends.

As Breslin left the court he swore he would kill McNally if he could lay his hands on him. He felt that he had been left out to dry. McNally knew that the case was flawed but hoped that the novice lawyer, Bradshaw, would not spot it. Now Breslin's own reputation was on the line. How could he get out of it, with at least some dignity?

Chapter 14

There was no let-up in the heatwave which had commenced in early July and was now in its sixth week and getting hotter. Restrictions on unnecessary use of water were the order of the day and air-conditioning units were at full output – for those who had them. Chief Ned Brennan didn't, and that didn't improve his humor as he sat facing Mary Donnelly, the District Attorney, in his sauna-like small office. The portable air-conditioning unit he had been given by maintenance was as useful as a lighthouse in a desert.

The ongoing work on the rebuilding of the station, while still ongoing, was in Ned Brennan's opinion, painfully slow. Hoping to hurry things up he had recently raised the issue with Jeff Suarez, whose company had won the contract for the job. However, Suarez had explained that trying to rebuild an old building in a very tight and busy part of Columba's Avenue, while it was still an operational police station, made it difficult to speed things up. Since then he had taken to personally visiting the site on alternate evenings when he could be seen viewing the progress while leaning on the scaffolding and looking out over the site while enjoying a cigarette. He would call the

Chief on a weekly basis and give him an up to date report on progress.

"What do you mean Mary? How could Alice Newman's divorce be in question? Has the place gone completely mad and who the hell is this Tim Bradshaw?" he roared.

"Remember Ned? He is the rookie lawyer appointed to act for Alice Newman. He looks the essence of incompetence, but he is as sharp as a razor," replied Mary.

Mary then recounted the conversation she had just had with Bradshaw on what had transpired in court that morning. Apparently the judge was looking for precedence in the case and had promised to give her ruling within days.

"Let's look at this calmly," said the Chief, as he tried to regain his composure. "It is bad enough to have Alice's incarceration questioned but now we also have her divorce. What the hell is going on?"

Wiping the sweat off his forehead he said. "OK, so let's look at the divorce issue. I assume that neither Party wants the marriage reinstated. They are both very happy to be apart from each other."

"Yes, that would appear to be the case. I would go so far as to say it is stating the obvious." Mary was the essence of coolness.

"If that is so then the reason for raising the issue now

is obviously a question of the division of the spoils, so to speak. Why not suggest to the judge that she get both parties together and see if they would agree to a more equitable division of the property while leaving the divorce decree intact."

"Do we think Gregg would go for that?" Mary asked. "After all, he has the most to lose."

"That may be the case," the Chief admitted, "but remember, from what was said in court today, he could be up for fraud or even perjury regarding the signing of the documents. That would delay the early release we had agreed with him when he turned state's evidence for us last year. It should be enough to convince him to be more amenable to an equal division of the assets. The one big stumbling block that I see is the question of custody of their daughter Tracey. I would suggest that until the big question of Alice's mental state is established, Tracey should be made a ward of court and remain living with her aunt. Maybe you could have a chat with the judge, off the record?"

"Yes, I think that might just work." said Mary, "If it does then the divorce decree stands and both parties get what they want. Alice's incarceration can be dealt with as a separate issue. I will call Judge Breen and suggest to her that she convene a hearing between both parties and their representatives, as soon as possible." said Mary.

"Are we ever going to see the end of the Newman saga?" asked the Chief. "And as if that isn't enough, now we have the added pressure on our resources with the annual regatta coming up and half of my force taking vacations at the same time," he exaggerated. "Everybody is trying to get away from the heat and if this keeps up until next weekend there will be no wind for the sailing competitions. What a mess!"

Immediately, on leaving the Chief's overheated office, Mary rang Joe Breslin to arrange a meeting. She then called the judge to apprise her of what she was doing.

The following morning, a somewhat subdued Joe Breslin arrived at the DA's office. Once the DA had reviewed the situation and outlined the proposed solution he had reverted to his usual brash manner and immediately went on the offensive.

"Are you seriously asking me to suggest to my client that he give that woman half of his total assets? And possibly give up custody of his daughter? No way!" said Breslin.

However, by the time the DA had pointed out the stark reality of Newman's position Breslin began to temper his objections. Eventually he agreed to consult with his client and get back to the DA within twenty-four hours.

The DA's next call was to Tim Bradshaw, who, unlike Breslin, appeared to be open to the proposal and welcomed an early meeting with Breslin and the DA

His only concern would be, he said, the accuracy of any disclosure of assets that Mr Newman might come up with; he didn't trust that man and sought assurances of support from the DA in this regard. The question of custody was not up for debate. Mr Newman had proven, by his misdemeanor and subsequent jail sentence, that he was not a suitable parent for Tracey. That was it, no debate.

By three p.m. that afternoon the DA got a call from Breslin to say that his client was open to discussing the proposal and that he, Breslin, would be available to meet with Bradshaw at her office at nine a.m. the following morning.

The following day, it took over three hours of haggling before both parties agreed to the division of the assets. Bradshaw, acting on behalf of Ms Newman, indicated that his client really didn't want any specific items as they would only remind her of the way life had been between herself and Gregg. However, he was not going to let Breslin see that and so appeared to fight to the bitter end over everything. On the other hand, Breslin obviously well briefed by Gregg, whose attachment to the symbols of wealth was well known, fought tooth and nail over everything. Once all the items were agreed on, it was decided that the house be sold. According to Bradshaw, Alice had no intention of ever living there. As for Gregg; well he was finished in Oakville and so, according to Breslin, he intended going west and starting a new life.

Once the main issues were thrashed out, it had been decided to let Tracey remain a ward of court and stay with her aunt for the immediate future, the DA called the judge to let her know the outcome of her mediation. The judge then contacted both parties to appear before her court on the Friday as previously arranged.

Every chance the Chief got he visited an office that had air-conditioning. And so as he sat, enjoying the air-conditioning in the DA's office, he said, "You know Mary, there are times when I get tired of trying to uphold the law. No sooner have we solved one problem, than two or more arrive on my desk. It never seems to end."

"That's the game we are in Ned." replied Mary. She'd heard it all before. It was the Chief's favorite rant.

"I suppose you are right. You know, I have a funny feeling that we haven't seen or heard the last of Tim Bradshaw. However, I firmly believe that we need someone like him to shake things up around here." said the Chief.

"You had better believe it. I hear he will be appearing on the upcoming and much publicized NTTV debate series on the question of psychiatric court committals. You know the one being organized by the Oldtown Chronical and NTTV. It's being hosted by that young reporter, Shirley Green, the one who was credited with finding Alice Newman."

"That should be interesting. Who else will be on the show?" asked the Chief.

"I'm not sure but I believe that apart from Don Harding, the Chronicle's editor, Butch Collins from NTTV and Doctor Bill Power from the Minerva Clinic; all of whom one would expect to be there. There is talk that our Mayor, Erin Sullivan, Tim Bradshaw and believe it or not, retired Judge Leo Forrest will possibly take part."

"Whatever the outcome," said the Chief, "it will help to keep this Newman-Lummox case in the headlines. We really need to catch a break on this."

"Maybe it will," said Mary. "But at least it might put pressure on the authorities to review the Alice Newman committal."

"Let's hope you are right." said the Chief. "Let's hope you are right."

Chapter 15

The following Tuesday, four hours before the debate was scheduled to commence, Shirley was pacing up and down the apartment like a hen about to lay an egg.

"Just be you and everything will be perfect." said Eddie. "You're a natural chatterbox and the viewers will love your innocent wit."

"But they are all experts on a subject that I know very little about. I don't want to make a public idiot of myself on my first chat show." She had been fretting like this all day. Eddie did his routine one more time.

"Remember, honey, it's a two-way street. They see you as the expert host and they are probably more nervous than you. After all they will be hoping that you don't ask them any questions that they can't or won't answer with certainty. Remember you are the ringmaster, you call all of the shots. And remember, you will probably never again get the chance to tell your boss, Butch, when, and when not to speak!"

"Eddie my love, I don't know what I would do without you. You always know the right buttons to press." But Shirley wasn't completely relaxed yet.

"One last piece of advice; get to the station in plenty

of time. I know that since last week the heatwave has died down somewhat, but it is still very hot out there. Just walking from the car to the door could have you in a lather of perspiration, even before you get to put on your TV face. You wouldn't want that now would you?" Shirley headed back to the shower, one more time.

By the time she arrived at the station she was still nervous but at least her professionalism was firmly in place again.

In setting up the format for the show, Shirley had insisted on having the participants seated in an informal and conversational manner around a table as if they were just there having coffee and discussing the topic among themselves, while she pulled the strings – when necessary.

Just before the show went live she addressed the panel members.

"Remember the rules," she said, trying to keep her voice normal while her heart was pounding in her chest. "I want you all to remember that we are here to try and solve a perceived problem – not score political points. I want just one voice at a time and of course keep it simple and no hogging the microphone. If you do, I'll just cut you off. Ok? I'll make sure everyone gets time to speak. I will commence with an overview of the problem, a copy of which you have all received. I will then ask our Mayor, Erin Sullivan, to start the debate. Finally, with ten minutes to go I will ask each of you to have a final say of about one minute each, before I wrap it up. We have just one hour, so let's go!"

To say that the show was a success would be the understatement of the year. Very little heat, but a lot of light, was produced and the phones and twitter never stopped ringing and tweeting long after the show had ended. As for Shirley, well she was just herself – the star of the show. She earned the somewhat begrudging praise from Butch: 'I suppose you will be looking for a pay rise now!' he said to her.

From the Mayor, Erin Sullivan, had come a very definite and public promise to act immediately on the problem.

The press reviews the following day were unanimous in opinion that it was a well-structured informative programme. The message coming from the debate was that it was now incumbent on the state legislature to immediately introduce a statutory review of all such cases. It did however point out that retired Judge Leo Forrest had not fully agreed with what was being proposed. Forrest had forcibly argued that in his view the introduction of any change, could not be retrospective. He felt that those who were already in the system, could, in his opinion, be addressed only on an individual basis and with the consent of all parties involved.

Some of the reviews had pointed out that Tim Bradshaw had countered by saying that it was because the judge himself actually had been responsible for many such committals, during his time on the bench. An argument which Forrest had rebutted by saying that judges could only act on medical evidence put before them. They couldn't just make up the law. Apparently Bradshaw wasn't buying this and ended up accusing Forrest of having vested interests in the whole issue. To which Forrest had replied that he wasn't going to be lectured by someone still wet behind the ears. It had taken an intervention by Shirley to calm things down. However, from there on both Bradshaw and Forrest sparked off each other with Forrest coming out the looser and doing his position little good.

"You wowed them mighty," said Eddie as he swung her off her feet, as she left the studio. "What a star performance! Honey you are on your way to stardom but don't forget who loves you baby! I only hope you won't get so busy I'll have to make appointments to see you."

"What's new mister! You have always had to do that, or didn't you know?" said Shirley smiling from ear to ear.

Oh God, I can see fame going to my head, I am getting a headache already."

"Come on, I think this deserves a celebration. I have booked the table at Mario's."

Chapter 16

Two days after the TV debate, Mayor Erin Sullivan, being true to her promise to act immediately on the problem, arranged a meeting in her office with Chief Ned Brennan, District Attorney Mary Donnelly and Doctor Bill Power with the purpose of setting up a Tribunal of Inquiry.

"Good morning and thank you all for coming at such short notice. The purpose of which is to bring you up to date on my promise to set up a Tribunal of Inquiry." said the Mayor. "I assume all of us have either attended or watched the debate. However, I am conscious of the fact that the Chief and DA were not privy to the off-camera tensions and nuances that went on around the debate."

"Well, both of us watched the replay again before coming here and we did pickup on some of the tension." replied Ned, "I do however appreciate that, off-camera there would have been a lot more that went on before and after the debate."

"Let me state from the beginning," said the Mayor, "the television program really opened my mind to the reality of what has been accepted up to now. I have given the matter a great deal of thought and have decided to ask retired Judge Ben Grillish, a renowned judge of the high court, to chair the tribunal. I have briefed him and his initial suggestion was that perhaps Doctor Power and Attorney Bradshaw would agree to sit on the tribunal with him. I can confirm that both have agreed to do so."

"That is just what we need and may I congratulate you on such a speedy and definite response." said the DA.

"Thank you." said the Mayor. "Now as I see it we have three distinct issues. Firstly, we have to resolve the case of Alice Newman's detention as a matter of urgency. Secondly we have to deal in some way with those already in the system. Finally, we have the issue of preventing a repeat of the travesty of justice that Alice Newman endured. These are the issues that the tribunal will be looking at. I have allocated one of my offices for tribunal meetings and Ben Grillish is already there waiting for Doctor Power and Mr Bradshaw to join him and commence his investigation."

Having led Bradshaw and Power into an adjoining room and introduced them to Grillish, then the Mayor left them.

Even though Judge Ben Grillish was only five foot five inches in height, he made up for it in width which gave him the impression of rolling as he advanced to shake hands with both men. However, whatever impression his size gave them was soon forgotten as he got down to business with a sharp and clear focus on the task in hand. Having summarized the details of the task as outlined to him by the Mayor he quickly got down to business.

"Let's take the case of Alice Newman first." he said looking at Doctor Power. "Where are we with it?"

Having outlined the review process necessary in the case, Doctor Power went on to say, "Right now I am prepared to initiate that review immediately. I have already contacted two out of state psychiatrists to examine her as soon as we agree to go ahead with it. All I need is your say so."

"And what is your opinion Bradshaw?" asked Grillish.

"I have no objection to that," said Bradshaw. "As a matter of fact, the sooner we do that the sooner Alice will be free. However, I have already mentioned to Chief Donnelly that we may be making a claim against the state for wrongful incarceration, on the grounds that the state is culpable for what she endured."

"You are? I'm aware that a recent court case has held that Doctor Mackey, on his own admission, was responsible for her incarceration." responded Grillish, "While on the other hand it must also be made clear to Ms Newman, and to you her attorney, that the police are still investigating an unsolved murder; a murder that Alice Newman may know something about."

"In the meantime, Doctor Power, can you arrange for Ms Newman to be assessed by your colleagues. When we have their report we can then take the next step. Remember we are looking in the first instance to establish the current state of her mind and secondly as to whether or not she was insane, as determined by the court, when she was initially committed."

"Now let's look at the second issue on our list. Namely, what do we do with those who are already in the system?" said Grillish.

"That second issue might be more difficult to remedy," said Doctor Power. "To remedy this we would need to establish who and where they are. To date any efforts to establish such details from clinics and courts, have been deflected by the phrase patient confidentiality."

"Ok, let's park that for today. Now the third issue, insuring that the practice does not happen again. Where are we on this?" asked Grillish.

"This is probably the easier of the three to resolve." said Bradshaw. "It simply needs a change in legislation to ensure that patients committed by court order must have a review of their case, carried out by independent psychiatrists, every three years."

"Will the legislators agree do you think?" said Grillish, looking enquiringly at Bradshaw.

"I would have high hopes." replied Bradshaw.

"Well let's see. I will draw up a petition and get the ball rolling." said Grillish.

The following Thursday Doctor Power rang Grillish to confirm that the assessment had been arranged for the following Monday at ten a.m. in the Minerva Clinic. Their report, he estimated, would take up to two weeks to complete and would be available about mid-September. By then Detective Inspector Eddie McGrane and others in the detective unit would be back from their summer vacations.

When Grillish called Bradshaw to notify him of the date of Alice's assessment, he immediately demanded that he be allowed to select one of the assessors. 'Why should the state be the final arbiters in the case?' he argued; after all it would be his contention that the state themselves had a case to answer. However, Grillish pointed out, that both assessors were independently appointed by Doctor Power on the instructions of the tribunal. If Bradshaw objected to their findings there was a procedure that he could follow.

Later, as Bradshaw spoke to Alice on the phone, he said to her, "If, at any point in the proceedings, you don't feel up to their questioning, don't hesitate to demand a recess, I am here to give you any advice you may need. This is your key to freedom – a freedom you richly deserve."

"Oh my God!" replied Alice. "I don't know if I can go through more questioning like that. You know, the psycho-babble kind? They can prove anything if they want to, you know?"

"Listen Alice," replied Bradshaw, "everything will be just dandy. I will have a talk with Doctor Power later on today and I will visit you before the end of the week when we will make sure you are fully prepared for anything they may ask. I do believe that you have nothing to worry about. We are all on your side really."

Chapter 17

Having been handed the report by Doctor Power earlier that morning the DA was now reporting it to the Chief. "Why do experts always couch their reports in language that most lay people don't understand?" she muttered.

"Forty-five pages of technical jargon about stress, trauma and grief, and many other issues that had or was or might be affecting Alice Newman." exclaimed the DA.

"Ok, give me the bottom line," asked the Chief.

"The bottom line appears to be – note I said, appears to be – that Alice Newman is as sane as you or I. The indications are that she was suffering from a nervous breakdown at the time of her committal; the breakdown being attributed to the behavior of her husband and fuelled by an overindulgence in alcohol."

"So that's it?"

"Well, yes and no. In between the forty-five pages are a lot of ifs and buts. The treatment she had received has apparently left her memory a little hazy in places. However, the suggestion is that these lapses of memory may be overcome in time by careful and gentle counselling or even by resorting to hypnotherapy."

"Does that mean that she is free to leave the clinic

immediately?" said the Chief, his eyebrows raised expectantly.

"Yes, Doctor Power is ready to sign her release, but with the recommendation that she attends the clinic for counselling once a week for an initial period of three months. This is to ensure that she is responding well to her new situation and not regressing in any way."

"Ok," said the Chief, "I will call Bradshaw and discuss it with him and remind him that it is our intention to question her regarding the death of Angie Lummox. I will suggest that he voluntarily present her here at the station rather than have us do it at the clinic. I think that would be better."

"Your idea that she presents herself here is a good one." the DA agreed. "In the meantime, I will call Bradshaw and arrange a meeting with him. It's better to keep him onside. He sounds as if he could make things difficult for us if he thinks that we might stray in any way."

"One other thing, has Alice met up with her daughter yet?" the Chief asked.

"No, I understand that Doctor Power had organized to have one of his youth counsellors visit Tracey on a number of occasions and on one such visit, she arranged for Tracey to speak to Alice on the phone. Apparently both are holding up well even though, according to the counsellor, the phone call was very emotional."

"By the way," added the Chief, "any idea where she intends to live when she leaves the clinic?"

"No idea. Apart from the people in the clinic, I don't suppose she has many friends around Oakville." the DA suggested. "She may even decide to go back to her original home up near Wayward Creek. If I were her, that's what I would do."

"We can't allow her go too far. She is now the only suspect we have and the circumstantial evidence against her is very compelling. What a mess Gregg Newman has created. Can you imagine what will happen if Alice, having just been released from the clinic is sent to jail for life?"

"Do you really believe she is guilty, Chief?"

"All I can say is that it doesn't look good. Bradshaw will have his work cut out for him. Anyway, I am glad that Eddie is back from vacation. As of tomorrow he will be back on the case fulltime."

Chapter 18

One of Eddie McGrane's strengths was his attention to detail. Everything had to be thoroughly researched and analysed before he made a decision. Now almost one year after first setting his eyes on Shirley Green, he knew without a single doubt, that she was one in a million. The one whom he wanted to grow old with, the one who was so good to be with, the one who made him forget his failed marriage and want to try it again. The one who had such real down to earth life values. They were so good together. Having returned from their vacation, Shirley and himself were enjoying a meal in Mario's. It was no surprise to his friends when he went down on one knee and asked her to marry him; with Dean Martin crooning Amore in the background, just as he had been on their first date.

"Eddie McGrane, get up and stop embarrassing me! Oh my God, are you serious? How am I going to be able to eat now? What am I saying? Oh Eddie, yes! Yes, I love you so much." said Shirley as she jumped up and threw her arms around him, spilling her drink in the process.

"Sit down woman for God's sake! People will think we are not the full nickel."

"Oh Eddie, I thought that nothing could be better than

our vacation. Being together all day, every day, for the full two weeks – but this! When did you get the courage to ask me? I was nearly despairing! I must tell mother. She will be thrilled. She says you're not too bad and that I could have done worse!"

"To be honest with you, I already asked her if I could have you – provided the price was right. She accepted a dollar, just to get you off her hands!" said Eddie with a smile on his face.

"You mean to tell me that you actually asked my mother for my hand in marriage? You old softy! You're perfect... well almost."

On cue, Giovani, the owner, arrived at the table with two glasses and a bottle of champagne.

"Hey Eddie, we thought you would never ask her. You certainly took your time about it. Anyway, since it was here to our very own restaurant that, you brought the girl who always lights up the place, for your first date one year ago, it is appropriate that you should propose to her here also. Congratulations and a long and happy life to you both." Giovani popped the cork and filled their glasses.

The rest of the evening was a haze of champagne and excitement. Thanks to social-media, word had gone around to all Eddie and Shirley's friends and they descended on Mario's in their droves. Even Butch, Shirley's boss at the station, arrived with his wife. As the night wore on the decked balcony over the lake became almost a floating bar.

"Eddie honey, I think I'm going to fall asleep," said Shirley in a somewhat slurred voice, "but I can't do that. We have so much to plan, haven't we?"

"We certainly have a lot to do, but not just now. I just remembered that I have an important meeting with the Chief at nine a.m. tomorrow morning. Oh my head! We'd better get home."

The following morning when Eddie presented himself at the Chief's office, he looked very much the worse for wear.

"You don't look like a person who has just returned from two weeks at the beach," were the Chief's first words to Eddie as he walked into the office. "You look and smell more like someone who was in a brewery for two weeks."

"I'm not as bad as I look, Chief," replied Eddie. "In fact I am far worse! But nothing that a few coffees won't cure. You see, it's like this Chief, I proposed to Shirley last evening and suddenly everybody wanted to celebrate. Mario's went mad."

"Well congratulations to you both. I think you are made for each other. Any plans yet?"

"Well Shirley was just getting around to that question

when I realized that the vacation was over and that I would be looking at other plans here in your office this morning; so no plans were made."

"Ok, let me lead you in gently Detective Inspector Eddie McGrane. Progress is being made on the new station, slow though it is. But, in the meantime I now have an office that fits more than four people. And it has a form of air-conditioning. From an operational point of view, we have been run off of our feet with a string of petty larcenies and, more worryingly, an increase in aggravated assaults on the person."

"How much of it is local and how much attributable to visiting trash?" asked Eddie.

"It looks like fifty-fifty, as far as I can see. As the city has expanded so has unemployment, so idle hands can be easily led astray."

"Is there any pattern in the petty larcenies?"

"No not really, but your partner has been looking into that area and I have a separate squad looking at the assaults. Thank God for CCTV. It's our savior."

"So what's been happening with the Angie Lummox case?" Eddie asked.

"Well the big news is that Alice Newman's divorce has been resolved. Both agreed to divide the assets equally and Alice to get custody of Tracey." said the Chief as he stood up and handed Eddie a bundle of files.

"So, Chief where does that leave Alice's mental state legally? Can we interview her?" asked Eddie.

"As you will see in her file the clinic had two independent psychiatrists assess Alice and according to their report she is deemed to be as sane as you or I. They also were of the opinion that at the time of her committal she was not insane but was having a nervous breakdown. She is now free to leave the clinic."

"Well that resolves that. Now we can start making progress with our investigation." said Eddie while putting the bundle of files back on the Chief's desk and starting to make some notes in his pocket note book.

"Exactly. I have spoken to the DA who has advised Alice's attorney, Tim Bradshaw that we see her as someone who may be able to help us with our investigation into the death of Angie Lummox and that we are going to proceed with our investigation. So drop everything else you may have on your desk and meet me here again tomorrow at the same time. Let me know how you plan to proceed. Now go and get some more coffee and take a walk around the block to clear your head. By the way, good luck to Shirley and yourself; you've got a very special one there, Eddie."

Having done what the Chief had suggested and

walked around the block a few times, Eddie felt his head beginning to reconnect with his body once more. Promising himself never again to drink champagne, no matter what the celebration might be. He called Lennie in forensics and Maria his partner, to a meeting in his office. Once the congratulations and questions of when, where and how, were dealt with Eddie said, "I have just had a meeting with the Chief and his instruction to me is that we drop everything we are doing and solve the Angie Lummox case. Just like that!"

"Does that mean that Alice Newman is now available for interview?" asked Maria.

"Yep, she has been pronounced sane and is free to leave the clinic immediately. A word of caution though, she has an attorney, Tim Bradshaw, and by all accounts he is a live one. And that is according to the DA. Also, the psychiatrists report mentions that she may be suffering from selective memory loss or confusion. So we must proceed with care."

"Let's hope her memory loss doesn't extend to the items we found in her room." said Lennie.

"Well she can't now deny that the black ski-suit and balaclava are hers; she already admitted that when we confronted her with them. It is the other items, particularly the documentation relating to micro cameras and the workings of car power steering and braking systems, that we need to focus in on." said Eddie.

"Funny thing is that while her fingerprints are all over these documents, there are other fingerprints also on them. However, when we carried out the fingerprinting of all of the staff at the clinic, there was no match." said Lennie.

"Are you sure you got everyone's prints?" asked Maria.

"Certain. From the matron down to the gardener, and the matron checked the numbers herself." replied Lennie.

Chapter 19

It was a few days before Eddie eventually managed to agree a time to get Alice Newman and her attorney to attend at his office. While acknowledging that Eddie and his fiancée, Shirley, were responsible for locating Alice, Bradshaw had initially insisted that his client be given a few months to rehabilitate before being interviewed.

However, when it was put to him that time was of the essence and that if needs be, she may have to be arrested as being a material suspect, he relented but promised to protect his client all the way. Eddie felt that the interview would be like walking on thin ice. As they prepared for the interview which was to be conducted by Eddie and Maria, Eddie said, "I think you should take the lead in the interview Maria. Alice will probably sense more empathy with you asking the questions. Her recent experience with men hasn't been good."

When Bradshaw and Alice arrived on the Friday morning, Bradshaw was dressed in a brown colored tweed suit with a matching waistcoat, as if trying to look like Gregory Peck in To Kill a Mockingbird. Once again his mop of blond hair looked as if it had not seen a comb for many a day, but he still kept brushing it back from his eyes with his fingers.

Alice, on the other hand, while still looking nervous and unsure of herself, was beginning to have some life in her eyes. She was dressed in a smart lavender colored two-piece linen suit and her hair appeared to have been given a different shade of grey. When she was found, her hair had been almost completely grey. They arrived and settled in, and were formally introduced to Eddie and Maria. Eddie thanked them for attending and said that it was noted that Alice was attending the interview of her own volition. He also said that it was appreciated that she was doing this with a view to helping the police with their investigation into the death of the young girl at her husband's home the previous year. A death for which the court had found him not guilty.

He then advised her that, for the protection of all concerned, and as was normal practice, the interview would be recorded on video.

While agreeing to co-operate in every way possible, Bradshaw reiterated his view that his client was the victim of a flawed judicial system and had been damaged by it. Any insinuation that she was involved in that unfortunate event would bring the interview to a sudden halt. After all she was attending on her own volition. Eddie and Maria decided to let that slide for the present.

"Ms Newman, we want to thank you for agreeing to

come here today," began Maria. "You have been through a very traumatic time. We appreciate that some of what we want to talk to you about, you may find upsetting. Please feel free to tell us if that occurs. We can take a break at any time."

"Thank you." said Alice in a very quiet voice.

"Now, if I can just bring you back to the interview we had with you in the Minerva Clinic, when we discovered who you really were. Do you remember that?"

"Yes, I do remember it very well. It was quite upsetting."

"And do you remember saying that you used to dress up in your black ski-suit and balaclava and, using the late Doctor Mitchum's car, you would break in to your husband's house on various occasions?"

"I never said that I broke in. I always believed that the house belonged in part to me, just as the Family Court has now decreed. And I always used the key he had left out for his lovers." Alice's face colored as she said this. Maria pretended to ignore Alice's embarrassment by looking at her notes.

"Ok, on the evening that Doctor Mitchum died in that terrible accident, the same evening that Angie Lummox died in your husband's house, do you remember visiting your house?"

"No."

"Is that a no you don't remember, or no you didn't visit the house on that evening?"

"No, I didn't visit the house on that occasion." Alice's gaze was steady.

Maria hesitated and stole a glance at Eddie. She hadn't expected Alice to deny what she believed to be true. After all Alice had already admitted in her earlier interview that, having borrowed Doctor Mitchum's car, she regularly visited the house. So why now deny it?

"Are you positive? How can you be so sure? After all, we know that you took Doctor Mitchum's car that evening and returned it just minutes before he left in it and crashed. So if you didn't visit the house, where did you go?"

"As usual I had intended going there, but when I got into the car there was a note on the dash."

"A note? What kind of note?" Maria looked at Eddie for a reaction. His face remained impassive.

"It just said that my daughter wanted to meet me, that I should park the car in the basement car park of the mall and she would meet me on the third floor outside the Pick and Chew café. But she never turned up."

"Was the note signed?" asked Eddie.

"No, it was a typed note but not signed by anyone. I was so excited at the thought of her wanting to meet me. I waited and waited. I almost forgot that I had to get the car back for the doctor. He was so good to let me borrow it, and now he is dead. I believe it is my fault entirely. If I had returned in time he wouldn't have been rushing home."

"Yes indeed," agreed Eddie, "that was a terrible tragedy but it was obviously a mechanical problem and not your fault in any way. You must have found it very upsetting losing such a special friend. From what I hear, he was very good to you. Now, if we can return to the note you have mentioned. Did you, by any chance keep it?"

"No, I may have left it in the car. I really can't recall."

"I think that is enough for today. Ms Newman is obviously upset at having to relive that awful evening." said Bradshaw.

"We very much appreciate that, Mr Bradshaw, but rather than bring Ms Newman back again to finish this area of questioning, perhaps you might let us probe just one other issue." replied Eddie.

"Very well, just one. Let's see what it is." said Bradshaw.

"Ms Newman, when we searched your room, under warrant, at the bottom of your wardrobe we found a number of items, including the clothing you have admitted to be yours. Apart from the clothes two of these items are of interest to us. Firstly, a number of computers printouts of the workings of power steering and braking systems of cars. Secondly, we found instructions for the working and installation of micro-security cameras. Can you explain to us why you had these items hidden in your wardrobe?"

"I don't know what you are talking about. These you say were in my wardrobe? If they were, then someone must have put them there!" exclaimed Ms Newman.

"Your fingerprints are all over them," said Eddie. "How do you explain that?"

"I simply can't explain it. I can see no reason why I would possibly have had them, unless I picked them up with other papers. I really have no explanation."

"OK that's it. This interview is over. My client won't answer any further questions." said Bradshaw, packing up his notes.

"Very well." Maria said. "We'll leave it there for now. We would ask that your client remain available should we need to ask further questions as the investigation progresses. Thank you for coming today. I'll see you to the lift."

As soon as they had left, Eddie and Maria were joined in the interview room by the Chief and DA who had been observing the interview from another room.

"Well," said the Chief, "what did you make of that?

Was it a good performance or was she telling the truth?"

"The doctor might have said that she was fragile but I didn't get that impression. She appeared to be fully focused and I think she was being honest with us." replied Eddie. "There was no sign of defensiveness or aggressiveness when answering Maria's questions."

"So where does that leave us?" asked the DA.

"It leaves us in a very difficult place," replied Eddie. "If what she told us is true, then she had nothing to do with the death. So who did? Secondly, why would someone send her off in a wild goose chase, knowing that her daughter wouldn't possibly be there? Finally, why would someone specify where she was to park the car – four floors below where the spurious meeting was to be? The plot thickens."

"Damn it!" said the Chief. "There is no way that CCTV records would still be held at the mall. So how do we prove that she is telling the truth?"

"I know that it is almost a year ago but let's assume that she is telling the truth. If we plot what route she would have taken from the clinic to the mall, maybe – just maybe – somewhere along that route we might find a CCTV recording for that time and date," suggested Maria.

"Good thinking," said the DA.

"Ok, we will get cracking on that immediately," said Eddie. "But while we are doing that I think we should also look at the implications if she is telling the truth."

"What do you mean?" asked the DA.

"Well the first thing we would have to look into would be; who put the note in the doctor's car? How did he or she know that Alice was trying to contact her daughter? Who knew that she would be using the doctor's car?"

"So what are you suggesting Eddie?" asked the Chief.

"I'm saying that if Alice is telling the truth, then we have a whole different scenario to investigate; including the fatal accident that killed Doctor Mitchum. If Alice Newman was not at the house on that evening and as Newman himself has been cleared. The question still remains: who did it and why?"

"Holy God! We appear to have opened a Pandora's Box!" exclaimed the Chief.

Chapter 20

It was slow and tedious work checking on every known CCTV camera along the four-mile route that Eddie had reckoned Alice would have taken to the mall – if she was telling the truth. A dedicated team of four officers had been seconded to Eddie's team for the sole purpose of checking every possible camera that might have held recordings for more than one year. Eddie had the luxury of being able to allocate a separate office for them to work in. Now, well into October, with the days getting shorter, not one single recording could be found. Most units had kept a maximum of six months' recordings and in some cases, only one month.

In the meantime, Eddie and Maria were looking into the possibility of some kind of conspiracy having taken place. Why would someone set Gregg Newman up for a murder and at the same time make sure that Alice wouldn't interrupt it by showing up at the house? "It would need inside information on both of their movements." Eddie suggested.

"Yes, and it would mean that someone at the clinic had the opportunity to put the note in Doctor Mitchum's car without being seen; someone who knew that Alice would be using the car on that very day."

"Yes, there definitely would have to have been a number of people involved. At least one person at the clinic and someone at the house." said Eddie as he made notes in his notebook.

"And what about at the mall, someone to make sure she didn't leave and turn up at the house?" Maria asked.

"Hold on to that for a moment," said Eddie while rubbing the back of his neck to ease the tension there. "There is another possible scenario. We never discovered what exactly happened to Doctor Mitchum. Why did his car go over the barrier and end up on the freeway in an inferno? Suppose it was not an accident? Suppose it was an attempt to kill Alice and not Doctor Mitchum? Just take that as a possibility and assume that the reason Alice was told to park the car in the basement level was so that someone could interfere with the brakes or power steering. On her way back to the clinic, Alice could have driven the car up to the clinic without using the brakes too often. However, it would have been a different thing when Doctor Mitchum would have had to use the brakes aggressively, coming down that hill in a hurry."

Eddie and Maria stared at each other, each building a mental image of the scenario.

"If we go down that road, we are really talking

conspiracy. So the next question we would have to ask ourselves is: why would anyone want to discredit Gregg and kill Alice? Why?" Maria waited for Eddie's response.

"Of course everything we have just come up with is pure speculation. We have absolutely no proof whatsoever to substantiate one single shred of it. That is apart from Alice's statement regarding the note she claims she found in the car." Eddie's hands were outstretched as Maria continued, "However, what if, on one of her visits to the house, Alice saw someone in the house. Someone who should not have been there? Would that be a reason to kill her? To keep her quiet?"

"There is also the question of the literature we found in her wardrobe. We never got a match for the second set of fingerprints we found on them. Did Lennie ever check to see if the printouts came from one of the printers at the clinic?" she asked.

"I don't know. We had better check. It is safe to assume that if they were printed at the clinic it would have been on a central printer so the chances of checking them back to a specific computer at this point in time would be zero."

"Hey Eddie, another thing we should look at, do you remember when we were checking where Doctor Mitchum parked his car? Remember we got a copy of the clinic's

CCTV which showed him running to his car on the evening of the crash? Do we still have the film?"

"I'm sure we do. It would be held in records."

"What I am thinking is that on that occasion, we were just confirming his departure and fast forwarded through hours of film. If we look again we might see someone putting a note in the car," suggested Maria.

"Good thinking. I will pull one of the guys off of the CCTV detail and get him to go through the clinic's own CCTV tape, inch by inch. They must be nearly finished checking every camera from the clinic to the mall by now and so far, have found nothing."

Later that evening as Eddie and Shirley were having dinner, Eddie was telling Shirley about their frustration of not being able to find any CCTV records anywhere that covered the evening in question.

"Have you checked the mall car park?" asked Shirley.

"Yep, there are cameras on every floor and outside but they only keep records for six months, unfortunately."

"No Eddie. I'm talking about the records of all cars entering the car park. You know as you come up to the barrier your registration number is scanned and I understand that these are stored on a year by year basis for analytical and financial returns reasons."

"Shirley Green you are an absolute genius! Why didn't any of us smart detectives think of that? Excuse me a minute, I have to make an urgent phone call," said Eddie as he jumped up from the table, rushed around to give Shirley a hug before going to find his phone.

"That's why we are so good together," said Shirley. "You help me and I help you. We are a team to be reckoned with!"

"Yeah," said Eddie, "but as we discussed, I can't tell you everything that goes on in an investigation whereas you have no such restrictions. That's going to be hard for us to live with."

The following day it took less than an hour for one of the squad to find that Alice had entered the car park at four thirty-two p.m. and left it at six p.m. She had been telling the truth.

Chapter 21

It had been another busy, hot and frustrating week for the Chief with plenty of leads and debate but no sign of a resolution to the Alice Newman saga. Just as he was about to clean off his desk and head home to pick up his wife and head off to join their hill-walking group for a weekend in the local mountains, he looked up to see Eddie standing at his door.

"OK, what's so important that you come knocking at my door at five p.m. on a Friday evening? I would have thought you would be off planning your wedding or something like that," said the Chief, as Eddie stood opposite him in his fancy new office. He had eventually agreed to move over to a temporary office in the building the detective unit was occupying. Now he had space and a proper air-conditioning system.

"I'm just about to spoil your weekend for you. Alice is telling the truth. She was at the mall on the evening in question, so she is out of the equation."

"Are you sure?" The Chief was incredulous.

"Yep. We found that the car park recording of cars entering and exiting the parking was intact. It showed her entering at around four thirty and exiting at about six p.m."

"What the hell! Where does that leave us?"

"It leaves us with a can of worms. That's what I think. Do you want to hear my theory?"

"Shoot. Get it over with and end my suspense."

"I believe that it was a conspiracy," Eddie began. "Someone wanted Gregg Newman out of the election and wanted Alice hidden in the psychiatric system but later, when she surfaced they wanted her dead. So the question is why? What did she do or what did she know?"

"You have jumped ahead of me Eddie. What makes you think someone wanted her dead? Where is that coming from?" said the Chief as he continued to file away the files from his desk, clearly indicating that he was not going to hang around unless it was urgent that he do so.

"Well, first of all let's look at the facts as we know them," said Eddie, advancing into the office. "Fact one: Angie Lummox was killed in Gregg Newman's home. Whoever did it, went to an awful lot of trouble to make it look like Gregg had done it. He has however been acquitted by the court. Now we know that Alice could not have done it either. So who did it?"

Having cleared his desk, the Chief sat down again.

"Fact two:" Eddie went on, "Literature relating to the braking and power systems of cars was found in Alice's room with her fingerprints on it plus the fingerprints of an unknown person, a person who did not work at the clinic. You remember that we checked all staff for prints and came up with zilch. Alice swears that she knows little or nothing about cars nor about the literature that we found in her room. I am inclined to believe her. So the question is - who put them there?

Fact three: the only time the car was unattended was when it was in the basement car park. Why was it there? Because whoever put the note in the car, wanted it in a place where it would be easy to interfere with it; far away from where Alice would normally park it if she was going to the third floor."

"Ok, I can't deny that you are making a very strong case for a conspiracy. So, assuming that, what next?" said the Chief in a tone that said: get on with it.

"According to my theory, someone at the clinic knew a lot about Alice and what her plans were. Someone there knew that she would be slipping out to take Doctor Mitchum's car and going to Gregg's house that evening. That someone put a note in her car. I believe that the purpose of that was twofold. One to keep her away from Gregg's house while he was being set up and secondly to give them the opportunity to interfere with the car, thereby killing two birds with the one stone – so to speak."

"You mean to say that Alice was the target and that Doctor Mitchum was an innocent victim?" The Chief was catching on fast.

"Yes, that depends on my theory holding water. Alice would have little use for the brakes heading uphill to the clinic but Mitchum would have relied on them very much coming down the hill, in his hurry home."

"So who do you think is behind all of this? Assuming that your theory is right?"

"As of this minute, I have no idea whatsoever," replied Eddie. "However, if my theory is right, then we have our work cut out for us with two murders to solve and the trail going very cold."

Realizing that Eddie was not going to drop the discussion, the Chief eventually asked him to sit down.

"And now you have ruined my weekend. Just when I thought that we were getting on top of things after the summer vacations."

"Well it's good that we have a little slack. It means that you can allocate a few extra foot soldiers to help us out with our enquiries. There is something in my head, not exactly an itch, that tells me that Alice has the answer but may not know that she has – if that makes sense."

"OK Eddie, in the absence of a better theory, I'll go along with you. Whatever resources we can spare, you can have them. Just remember that according to the report Alice is fragile and may be suffering from selective memory loss, so treat her gently."

"Memory loss or not, we have to try and get inside her head. I bet Doctor Mitchum did. I wonder did anyone else at the clinic get inside her head? That's where we must start, back at the clinic."

"Ok Eddie, unfortunately I have a prior commitment for the weekend. I suggest that we meet here first thing on Monday and formulate a plan."

Having returned to his own office Eddie phoned the clinic and explained to Matron Sue Smyth that they needed some further information on Alice Newman's stay at the clinic. He had agreed to call to see her on the following Monday morning. Now as Eddie and Maria headed back up the twisting and steep avenue to the clinic, they were again viewing the scene of Doctor Mitchum's accident but this time with a different focus. Eddie now firmly believed that it was the scene of a murder and not an accident.

As soon as they arrived they were immediately shown to the matron's office. As they sat down, Maria began. "Thank you so much for seeing us at such short notice. We just need to get your view on Alice's attitude to the other patients and also to the staff. Firstly, if I may ask, how do you think she related to the other patients?" asked Maria.

"Alice was always slow to connect with others," replied Matron Smyth. "She very much kept to herself. Indeed, it was one of the areas that I tried to get her to concentrate on. I even asked assistant matron Jane Starling to help. Do you remember her? She was excellent. Unfortunately, we lost her to a higher bidder. She is now with the Haven Clinic. Anyway she tried to get Alice to participate in communal activities but Alice only seemed to click with her own yoga classes. Which, as you know she ran so well. I suppose she felt in control of those classes and it did wonders for her confidence. Doctor Mitchum was very proud of that success."

"So you are saying that she really had no obvious confidante here other than Doctor Mitchum," asked Eddie.

"Maybe it could be possible without you knowing it?" suggested Maria.

"I doubt it very much," replied Matron Smyth, "You see, we are really a very small integrated community here and it would be very difficult for one of us not to notice any such relationship."

"Ok, but would the same apply to non-staff relationships." asked Maria.

"Even more so; she kept very much to herself ninety per cent of her time here, that is apart from her sessions with Doctor Mitchum and when she was holding her yoga classes."

"Just a question on her sessions with Doctor Mitchum, did she ever have sessions with any other psychiatrist during her time here with you?" asked Eddie.

"Absolutely not. Once, when Doctor Mitchum had to spend a week up at the capital, we tried to get her to continue her therapy with another excellent psychiatrist but to no avail. She wouldn't hear tell of it."

"One final question Matron, how many people would have had access to Alice's room?"

"Well, mainly we see a patient's room as his or her sacred space but of course we had to have visibility into the room at all times to ensure the patients safety. You probably observed the small window beside each door. In addition, we have a cleaning service and canteen service if a patient is unwell and unable to join the other patients in the restaurant."

"So, in fact it would have been quite possible for someone to leave unwanted periodicals or magazines in the room for the cleaners to tidy up scattered papers and place them in cupboards." asked Maria.

"Yes, that would be possible but why do you ask?"

"Well it appears that when our people searched her room they found a variety of articles on subjects that Alice claims that she knows nothing about. Your explanation would seem to clear that up for us. Anyone could have left them there." said Maria.

"As I mentioned," replied matron, "we are very protective of our patient's privacy and would be very annoyed if we felt that anyone was interfering with it. Now that she will be leaving us we will be very sorry to see her go but happy to hear that she is initially going back to Oldtown...."

"Oh, we didn't know that," said Maria. "When was that decided?"

"Sorry, I probably shouldn't have mentioned that. I assumed you would have heard of it. However, as she is now released from the clinic, she is free to go where she pleases. She specifically requested that what she did once she left the clinic was to be her business only. I do know that where she will be staying is being kept very quiet. She does not want the press camped outside her door."

"We appreciate your position Matron and no doubt her attorney has been in touch with our office to advise us of her where about." said Eddie covering his embarrassment at not knowing where she was, a prime suspect in the case.

Just as they were preparing to leave, Eddie turned and, as if it was an afterthought, said, "One other thing you might be able to help us with, I hate to impose on your time but if you could do this one final thing for us it would be of great help. You may remember that when we were investigating Doctor Mitchum's death we took copies of the CCTV tapes of the car park. Well we are now looking at them from another aspect. We are examining the tape that shows the area where Doctor Mitchum's car was parked on the day he died and trying to identify those who were in the vicinity of the car from two thirty p.m. and four p.m. There were not many and we have been able to identify about fifty per cent of them. We would appreciate if you would have a look at the tape when you have time, it would be of great help. If you agree I will have the tape dropped up to you. We have marked the places on the tape that we want you to look at so it should only take a few minutes of your time."

"Certainly, I will look at it as soon as you get the tape to me," replied matron.

"If it's ok with you, I will drop them into you tomorrow morning. It should take no more than thirty minutes for us to view them. Is that ok with you?"

At nine o'clock the following morning Eddie was at the door of the clinic with the tapes in his hand.

Twenty minutes later, having viewed the tapes, all those on the tapes had been clearly identified. That was, all except for one person who had crossed from the side of the clinic to where the car was parked. The car itself could not be properly seen as a delivery van was obstructing the view. Furthermore, it was hard to identify the person as he or she was using a golf umbrella and while it was not raining at the time, it had been raining earlier. Matron however opined it was a female but could not be sure. She said that there was something familiar about the walk but couldn't say what it was. In fact, what she had said was exactly what Lennie Bareman from forensics had said. He was sure that it was a woman; a woman who didn't want to be identified, hence the umbrella.

"Another dead-end," said Eddie as they got back to the car. "We need a breakthrough and we need it fast."

Chapter 22

The weather all year had been unpredictable. June, July and most of August had been swelteringly hot. September followed with almost constant rain and wind, if not every day, at least every second day. Now nearing the end of October it had changed to dry sunny weather again. According to Eddie, it was ideal barbeque weather. Dressed in a pair of white sports shorts, showing off his well-tanned legs, the result of his two weeks' vacation, and a multi-colored short sleeved shirt, he was now happily humming 'In the Summer-time.' He wasn't renowned for his singing. Though he kept turning the burgers and chicken fillets on the flame. All the while Shirley was multi-tasking, busily mixing salads while having an in-depth conversation on the phone with her mother about the wedding plans.

"But Mom, anything I might buy now might be either out of style by this time next year or, heaven forbid, it may not fit me." The wedding was planned for the Fall of the following year. "What do you mean? Are you telling me something I don't want to hear?"

"No Mom, of course I am not pregnant! If I get fat, it will be because my darling Eddie insists on cooking half pound burgers plus sausage and chicken for me to eat. He feels aggrieved if I don't eat them all, just like you used to say to us when we were kids. Remember Mom? 'Eat every piece before you leave the table or you will get it again for breakfast'."

Just then her cell phone rang. "Must go Mom, my cell phone is ringing. Call you tomorrow," said Shirley as she finished the call.

"Who did you say is calling?" asked Shirley as she headed into the kitchen in order to hear the call clearer, "I don't believe it! Kaley Brown. But of course I remember you. You were so friendly and helpful to me when I was lost in Oldtown."

Fifteen minutes later, having dismissed Eddie with a wave of her hand on at least three occasions, she emerged from the kitchen, red faced and beaming from ear to ear.

"The burgers are probably overdone and the rest of the food is probably gone stone cold, honey," began Eddie but stopped when he saw the look in Shirley's eyes. "Who was that, may I ask?"

"Oh Eddie, you won't believe it. I'm so lucky. I always said that since I met you everything seems to be going my way, like Oklahoma."

"Stop teasing me and tell me who or what has happened?"

"Well, do you remember when I went to Oldtown

looking for Alice Newman? On one occasion I located the house where she had lodged. The landlady's name was Kaley Brown."

"Yes I do, you referred to her as 'call me Kaley.' A very nice lady you said."

"Yes, that's the lady. Well that was her on the phone and – wait for it – she has a new lodger who has just arrived and who wants to meet up with me! It's none other than Alice Newman! Would you believe it? Every reporter worth her salt would give their eye teeth just to meet her. Oh my God, wait until I tell Butch!" gushed Shirley.

"Wow, you certainly are getting the breaks!" quipped Eddie

"I'll be heading south first thing in the morning and will see where things go from there. I don't suppose she will allow me a formal interview as yet, but hopefully she will give me first shot when she is ready. I might even put in a good word for you if the opportunity arises!" quipped a very happy Shirley.

"You're so good to me, you are all heart! Now honey, are you interested in eating some of this beautiful food?"

Later on as they sat watching a late film on TV, Eddie got to talking about Alice Newman and the fact that he knew so little about her relationship with her husband Gregg before they married. Did she socialize with his friends? Was she a part of their political pack? At what stage did she fall out of favor with them?

These were the things he needed to know but was not in a position to ask at the moment. Now Shirley had been given the key to the door and maybe, if the opportunity arose she might be able to get some answers.

One of the big issues that Eddie had to wrestle with in his relationship with Shirley was, how much of his work as a detective could he disclose to her and how much of the information he got from Shirley, in her role as investigative reporter, could he use. They were both very conscious of the tight-rope they were on but were determined to respect each other's position.

"It all depends on how Alice receives me," said Shirley. "From what Kaley said on the phone, she wants to meet the person who found her so that she can thank her in person."

Shirley's return to the home of Kaley Brown in Pine Street was a joyous occasion. Kaley, not in keeping with the weather wore a bright floral dress which would be more suited to a Hawaiian hot summer's day than for this time of the year, and hugged her as if she was a long lost daughter returning home. Alice, for her part was quietly excited.

"How can I possibly thank you for what you have done?" said Alice.

"Just seeing how happy you both appear to be is thanks enough for me." said Shirley.

Immediately Kaley boiled some water and announced that she had even baked an apple pie for the occasion. "You must have some of my special apple pie and ice-cream," she gushed. "It was Alice's favorite treat when she was lodging with me," and turning to Alice and giving her a hug she said, "isn't that so Alice?"

While Kaley busied herself in the small kitchen, Alice and Shirley made small talk. Alice was anxious to find out where Shirley came from, what kind of job she had and if she was married or not. When she heard that she had just become engaged to a detective she wanted to know all about their plans and was disbelieving when Shirley said that apart from a possible Fall wedding date, they had no plans. They were, according to Shirley, very happy as they were, so why complicate it? However, she insisted that when the day came, Alice would have to come to the wedding.

Once the coffee had been poured and generous portions of pie ladled onto their plates, the atmosphere relaxed and the conversation flowed without strain. Kaley was so overcome with the emotion of having Alice back with her that she was in danger of talking herself into breathlessness. She hardly ever came up for air as she reminisced about the good times they had together when Alice came to lodge with her. As for Alice, well she revelled in the comfort and security of being with her old friend. On the other hand, Shirley was caught between empathizing with the two friends while being conscious of her boss's last words to her; 'don't come back without an exclusive interview!'

"What was Oldtown like to live in when you first came here?" asked Shirley.

"To us country folk, Oldtown was the main town on the lakes, situated as it was on the southern tip of the lower lake it had everything going for it. Then suddenly the freeway came through the county and everything changed. Oldtown went into decline and Oakville on the northern tip of the upper lake began to blossom." said Kaley.

"Was it that sudden?" asked Shirley.

"To some it was." said Alice. "But when I married Gregg two years later, I very soon knew it was coming. The Pack was active."

"What do you mean by The Pack?" asked Shirley.

"You know, there are always the movers and the shakers in every change. The people that I mixed with when I married Gregg seemed to be well clued in to what was happening. They certainly didn't seem to be averse to it. As a matter of fact, most of them were very happy to move their business to Oakville. I personally wasn't happy with the prospect of transferring there with Gregg. However, he was going whether I was happy with it or not. I wasn't, as you know."

"Yes it must have been a terrible time for you." said Shirley. "Are you sure you want to continue talking about it? I don't want to upset you." said Shirley.

"I'm ok. It's just that when I remember how it was with my husband and his colleagues, I get so angry. At any time of the day or night they would descend on our house like a pack of wolves. That was what I used to call them, The Wolf Pack."

As Alice seemed reluctant to expand on The Wolf Pack, Shirley decided to let it drift for the time being. Alice then changing the topic away from The Wolf Pack said, "Kaley tells me you are spearheading a campaign to change the way patients who have been committed by the courts are held. Is that true?"

"Well it is really my boss at NTTV, Butch Collins and Don Harding the owner of the Oldtown Chronicle who are promoting the campaign. I have a very small part in it."

"But it was you who instigated it, wasn't it?"

"Of course it was!" interjected Kaley, "Since the day she found out who you are, she has been on the TV trying to get people to listen to the problem."

"Has there been any progress?" asked Alice.

"Yes, I think we have created a certain amount of debate on the issue but we need to create more."

"So how will you proceed? Is there anything I can do to help? Remember I have been a victim of the system and only for you I would still be there! I would really like to do whatever I possibly can," said Alice.

"Well there is something you could do, but to be honest I am slow to ask you at this point in time. Perhaps at a later date when you have had more time to adjust to your freedom, you might allow me to interview you for NTTV?"

"Thanks for your concern, Shirley, but I am good to go now," said Alice, her voice showing her emotional state. "I feel that the sooner people feel my pain, the sooner someone will listen. I think that this would be a great opportunity for me to let people know what it was like for me to be so helpless."

"If you are sure, I will arrange it immediately," said Shirley. "I totally agree with you that we need to hear you and to hear you all the way to the Governor's office. Then and only then will we get a proper answer. The Governor's office has been sitting on this for almost five years ever since Doctor Mitchum first wrote to them."

"Yes, I am very sure. Just say where and when," said Alice.

"Great," said Shirley, while trying to conceal her excitement. "Let me check with my boss and I will call you here at Kaley's number. I would suggest that we, very discreetly, do the interview in the station in Oakville. We don't want to publicize your whereabouts. That way we keep your location safe."

Chapter 23

As soon as Shirley got into her car she rang Eddie to tell him the news. His response was, "Fantastic! Well done but keep your feet on the ground and your eyes on the road. Please get home to me in one piece!"

Her next call was to Butch who was so excited, she was initially afraid he would have a heart attack. When he eventually calmed down he said, "Fantastic! Well done! Oh boy! As soon as you get back, get working on your script. We will have to reschedule Wednesday's programs to include a one-hour special Chat with Shirley program. Call into me the minute you get back and well done again."

When Shirley got back to Oakville she went straight to the station where Don was still in a state of excitement.

"How did you do it? You keep springing these surprises on me Shirley and you aren't even a fully trained reporter! Now that you have cracked it, I think both Don and I should be in on the interview. Just to show a united approach. You of course will introduce the program."

"Firstly boss, I don't believe that you need to be trained to use your common sense. She is just like me, a woman. She wants justice and she needs to talk. But we do need to be careful how we conduct the interview."

"What do you mean?"

"I think that the right way forward is to treat the interview as a human interest story, not a coup. A story that will resonate all the way up to the Governor's office. So I think Alice and I should be alone in a gentle setting, maybe having a cup of coffee and chatting. I think any kind of razzmatazz would destroy the potential this has to really make a difference. Anyway guys on it would frighten her off, in my opinion."

For a moment Butch was speechless. Was Shirley now telling him what to do? However, before he could react, Shirley said, "Isn't that what you were teaching me to do? To come up with a plan and then put it to you as my considered opinion?"

'Of course she is right.' thought Butch as he responded, "Ok, when you have all the pieces put together, run it past me and we'll see. By the way, well done."

Later that night she admitted to Eddie that she didn't remember driving home from Oldtown. All the way home her mind had been working overtime on getting her script ready. They were sitting by a nice log fire, the evenings having turned cool, celebrating with a bottle of wine and a take away that Eddie had ordered, while she shared her interview plans with him.

For Shirley the following day was taken up with preparations for the interview. Butch was not completely happy to entrust Shirley with the responsibility of such an important interview. But Shirley just told him to back off, that he was unnerving her. He took the rebuff with humor. He knew when to back off remembering how good she was, in her own simple fashion.

And good she was. Every detail from the studio background to the color of both Alice's and her own outfits were to be co-ordinated. No fear of a clash here. Having discussed the options, it was agreed to keep it simple and use gentle colors, nothing flashy. When those details were sorted out Shirley had suggested that on the day of the interview Alice would meet her for lunch and then they would drive to the TV station for rehearsals.

Ever since Shirley had told Butch that Alice was agreeable to do an interview for NTTV, he had gone into overdrive to ensure maximum coverage for the event. At least ten times a day he had continuity announcers advise viewers of the upcoming interview. Once again the small TV station was going to lead the way and once again it was Shirley who had made it possible. Now, if he could only convince her to ask the hard questions of Alice, he would be more relaxed. But Shirley was not for turning; she knew how far to push Alice without closing her down. And so it proved as the interview was recorded three days later. "You were absolutely great." said Shirley, to Alice, once the microphones had been turned off, "How do you feel?"

"In two words, exhausted but satisfied."

"I know we covered a lot of questions. I think the viewers will have got a very real sense of what it was like to be helpless, at the mercy of a system that had the right to sedate you at their will."

"Hopefully, but what about the rest of the interview? How did that go?"

"Personally, I was always curious to hear of your early days with Gregg and how his ascent into power politics affected you and your daughter. I think that you gave great insight into that as well. However, I feel that some viewers may have a difficulty in understanding how and why you put up with the constant visits of what you call The Wolf Pack to your home and how it may have affected your marriage."

"Yes, when I think back on those days I think of what our lives would have been like if Gregg had not fallen in with that group." Alice mused. "When it started we thought it was so exciting; Gregg being accepted into such a powerful political group, money beginning to flow and Gregg's future was heading skyward."

"There is something I wanted to ask you but decided it might have been too awkward to ask on air, how did The Pack originate and where did they get their money?"

"Well I'm glad you didn't ask that one because I don't know the answer to either question." Alice replied. "I think that at an earlier time in their careers, they were all members of the local health and sports center and graduated to the local golf and country club where they seemed to have common interests, mainly having fun and scheming about how to make money."

Just then Butch and Don arrived in to add their praise and thanks. According to Butch the phones and twitter comments were full of praise for Alice and her honesty and for Shirley and the way she had handled a very delicate interview; her star continued to climb!

"We already have a really good front page spread set for tomorrow's edition of the Chronicle. That should create additional interest in our campaign," interjected Don.

That evening Alice agreed to join Shirley and Eddie for dinner at their place and to stay with them for the night. It was agreed that first thing in the morning Shirley would drive Alice back to Oldtown.

Shirley had warned Eddie not to interrogate Alice, and in spite of his obvious anxiety to ask her questions, he surprised Shirley by not once mentioning her past experiences. Every subject he broached had to do with her future and where she hoped to go and what kind of values she would hope to pass on to her daughter. Once Alice got on to that topic the conversation flowed.

"Eddie McGrane, you certainly surprised me tonight with your empathetic conversation. It was like listening to the master at work," said Shirley as they settled down for the night. Alice having decided on an early night, had retired to their unfinished box-room.

"My secret is that I have been taking lessons from the master herself, Shirley Green the undisputed queen of the TV screen and master interviewer. You are the very best."

"Thank you, honey, but I doubt that you learned it from me. I think it's the other way around. I have watched you at work and you certainly know how to unlock people's minds."

Now that they were finally on their own Shirley was full of questions. What did he really think of the program? Did he think that her questions were balanced enough? How did he think that Alice came across to the viewers? Did she look nervous?

"The show was a masterpiece," said Eddie, taking hold of her hands. "Everything, from the setting to your performance, everything was spot on."

'But… I hear a but somewhere. But what?"

"I'm not too sure exactly what it is. As I said everything seemed just right. Alice got her pain and a very controlled anger across very well. But I think that when you were questioning her about her early days with Gregg that there was a big elephant in the room. She seemed to gloss over it too easily."

"Well bearing in mind that the objective of the program was to let people see what we are fighting for…. to see someone who went through that awful experience, I suppose I didn't see the need to probe any other issue."

"No honey, I am not criticising you. It is just that I found that situation very interesting. As a matter of fact, I think there is at least another program for you on the whole issue of how Oakville became the second city in the state when the obvious choice would have been Oldtown."

"Now that's a different kettle of fish, so to speak. What a brilliant idea mister detective! Good thinking."

"If you think it appropriate and Alice is willing, you might broach the subject with her as you drive her home tomorrow. Try and find out a little more about The Wolf Pack and any other names that she might remember."

"Yep, The Pack seemed to have been all consuming in their lives. That could be interesting."

"That would be putting it mildly. I think what Alice

is alluding to is more than just interesting. We, either you or I, need to push her on it. How do you feel about that?" replied Eddie.

"We couldn't do that Eddie. Alice is still very fragile and it has taken me all I could do to gain her trust. No, sorry Eddie but we can't go down that road right now."

"Okay, I suppose you are right. It's just that I feel that she has the key to understanding all that has happened." said Eddie

Chapter 24

The Monday morning meeting with his Chief was a sobering one for Eddie. Six weeks back from his vacation and none of the cases he had on his desk had progressed one iota. His theory regarding Angie Lummox's death had run into stone walls everywhere the squad had turned. He was beginning to doubt himself and his theory.

"I can understand why someone wanted Gregg discredited in order for someone else to get elected." Eddie said, conscious of the Chief's gaze. "But the Democratic candidate did win the election. So if it was someone from the opposition who did it, they didn't succeed. But why try and kill Alice? She had been out of circulation for over three years. Is it something she knows that could damage someone if it became public? Could it be something that she revealed during therapy?"

"That's a lot of questions Eddie, but have you any concrete answers? Or even a solid lead?" replied the Chief.

"No, at this point in time we are at a standstill, so we are going back to the beginning. We are particularly looking back on the transcripts of the case against Gregg Newman. One of the main tactics used by his legal team was to put doubts in the jury's minds regarding the possibility that someone in dark clothes was seen on many occasions near Newman's house at that time. At the time all we did was to try and discredit them."

"Yes," the Chief agreed, "and as Alice had admitted to visiting the house on many occasions, while dressed in black, we assumed that the person was her."

"Precisely, so now we have to examine the witness statements and correlate their sightings with Alice's statement to see if it gives us anything further to go on. We are really clutching at straws." Eddie's frustration was plain to see.

"Let's look at it from another point of view," said the Chief while doodling on his desk pad. "If someone was trying to connect Alice to the murder by planting the micro camera leaflet in her room, then there must be someone in the clinic that had inside knowledge on Alice's movements and had access to her room."

"But we checked the fingerprints of everyone at the clinic. It would have to be an outsider." replied Eddie.

"Did you check Matron's prints?"

"Yes, no one was left out. We checked everything against the staff list to be certain that we had everyone, and there was no match."

"Wait a minute. When did you carry out the fingerprint check?"

"I haven't the exact date but Lennie and his team did it in the last month or so."

"Don't you think you had better go back and check to see if any of the staff had retired or left the clinic between the time we found the documents and the time Lennie did the checking?"

The Chief was now looking pointedly at Eddie accusingly.

"If we missed that, we are slipping up big time. That should have been obvious. I will call Lennie immediately."

Eddie decided to leave the office before things got worse.

When he managed to contact Lennie and put the question to him he was relieved to hear that Lennie had asked that question and matron had assured him that all staff was accounted for. Nobody had left in the intervening period.

Later on, Eddie recounted the near miss with Maria, "We need a break!" he exclaimed.

"But what about the assistant matron, Jane Starling? I remember Matron telling us that she had gone to the Haven Clinic." Maria flicked back through her note pad.

"Wasn't that subsequent to the checking, or was it? I had better call Lennie and double check with Matron."

When Eddie got through to Lennie, he got his answer.

"Damn it!" said Lennie, "I remember that at that time Starling was on vacation and when I went back to get her later, she was no longer employed by the clinic, so we had no way to get her prints unless we did it surreptitiously. Bearing in mind her position at the clinic, I felt that we didn't have the authority to do it."

"OK, Lennie," said Eddie, "I'll take a trip up to the Haven Clinic and see if Starling is willing to have her prints checked. If she refuses it could mean that she has something to hide. I'll call her first to make an appointment to see her on some other issue."

The following morning, having arranged to meet Jane Starling at eleven thirty, Eddie and Maria headed north on the two-hour journey to the Haven Clinic to meet her. Not wanting her new employers to see her being interviewed by the police, Starling had requested they meet at the local Starbucks, which was ok with Eddie. At least the coffee would be good there!

As they approached the entrance they met Starling and selected a booth at the rear of the café.

"So what made you decide to leave the Minerva and come all the way up here?" Maria asked by way of an icebreaker.

"Well I was five years at Minerva and matron there has at least another ten years to go to pension and I thought that was too long for me to wait to take over. Here the gap is only three years. We have to plan for the future – don't we?" she smiled.

After a few further minutes of general chat, Eddie said, "I assume you want to know why we wish to talk to you. Well in fact all we need is to close the book on one aspect of our investigation into Doctor Mitchum's crash. While you were on vacation we fingerprinted all the staff at the clinic just to eliminate them from a certain aspect of the investigation. Apparently the Doctor's watch, which Beth had given him for a special occasion, was missing from his personal belongings when the clinic handed them over to her."

"Fingerprint! But why would you do that?" said a somewhat shaken Starling.

"Of course you don't have to do it if that is a problem for you." said Eddie. "We just need to eliminate you from the enquiry. All of the other staff had no problem with doing it."

"Of course I have no problem with it and want to be as helpful as I can, but, I think I would like to discuss it with my attorney first. I will let you know what he says. Now if that is all you need me for, I had better get back to work before someone sees us and thinks the police are after me!" Starling gathered her bag and coat and wished them good day.

Eddie and Maria looked at each other and simultaneously looked at Starling's unfinished coffee. Careful not to smudge any prints, Maria emptied the remaining coffee into her own mug and discreetly placed Starling's mug in a plastic evidence bag and slipped it into her own handbag.

As they drove back to Oakville, Maria asked Eddie what he made of the meeting and Starling's reaction.

"The first thing that struck me was the way she looked when she walked into the café." said Eddie. "She looked like a younger version of the drab and severe looking woman that I had remembered meeting at the Minerva."

"Amazing – that's just what I was thinking." said Maria. She definitely looked a different person. A bit of make-up and a change of hair style; what a difference it makes."

"However," resumed Eddie, "the second thing was her reaction. She froze when we told her why we were there. She is guilty of something. But what is it? Is she having an affair?"

"If she was the person at the clinic feeding the information on Alice's progress to someone else. Possibly the person who was at Gregg's house. We need to establish the connection. Who is that person?"

"Now that she has moved to the Haven up in Wayward Creek and that Alice is free, she may have dropped her guard a little." said Maria. "Let's check out her contacts in Wayward. I think she might have hidden so much here where she would have been in the limelight. Whatever it was she certainly disguised her appearance."

When they got back to the station they handed the mug to Lennie to check the prints. Two hours later they had a match. It matched the print on the documents discovered in Alice's room in the clinic. Now what to do with it?

At a hastily convened review meeting in Eddie's office later that evening the extra officers the Chief had allocated were divided into team. Each team was given a specific task or area to be responsible for. Team A was to check out the area where Starling used to live in Oakville, calling on neighbors and shops to establish who her visitors were and what her purchases were. Team B was to check her phone records in Oakville and in Wayward Creek. Team C was to check her bank accounts.

"This is urgent but above all it needs to be discreet, at this point in time we don't want to scare her off. She is the only link we have, so don't spook her. Good luck." said Eddie.

In the meantime, Eddie was to contact Doctor Moody up in Wayward Creek and see if he knew of Starling and possibly where she was living. Maria agreed to call the local police and get their input.

Doctor Moody, still enjoying the afterglow of his triumphant court battle with Mr Hemmingway, was delighted to get a call from Eddie.

"What a pleasant surprise, Detective!" was the doctor's opening remark. "I was beginning to think that my usefulness to humanity was at an end. Nobody to talk to and all day to do it – as my dear mother used to say before she passed away. She was ninety-five, you know. As clear as a whistle right up to the day she folded her tent. A great woman. Anyway I wander as usual. Now what can I do for you today?"

When Eddie had explained what he was looking for the doctor appeared to be rejuvenated. "Up here they don't call me 'nosey' for nothing. I can see the grass growing and hear the field mice chatter. Leave it with me, my man, and I should be back to you within twenty-four hours."

Maria wasn't so lucky. The station sergeant in Wayward was in a foul mood and made it very clear that he didn't have the resources to take on any additional work – especially for someone from Oakville. Two years earlier, in a move he considered sideways, he had been transferred from Oldtown to Wayward, which was in his opinion was a one horse town. It did however have a very large college student population and in his opinion college students equated with social misbehavior. He didn't like kids with too much of their parent's money to spend and too much energy. "No I don't know anything about a Ms Starling. Never heard of her and, before you ask, I don't have someone to go out and have a look. Thank you and good luck."

By the end of the week it became obvious that in Oakville, Starling was exactly what she looked like – a drab and friendless woman who, apart from her work, went nowhere and did nothing. It was either that or she was adept at covering her tracks. However, in Wayward Creek she was something different. She presented herself as a confident well-groomed young lady.

Two days later, as promised, Moody was back to Eddie with his report. According to it, Starling had either rented or purchased a beautiful detached bungalow about half a mile from where he lived. "Houses like that don't come cheap," he said, "and I believe it is fully furnished already."

"Any sign of a partner, male or female?" asked Eddie.

"Well, at my age I don't go out much at night and there is no activity during my daytime trips. However, the local store tells me that she is going to be a good customer. They are delighted of course. Apparently she has already ordered a large quantity of their best wine and beer and enough food to feed a large family. Looks like our Starling is preparing to entertain somebody special! I'll keep you posted."

Team B reported that it was not possible to get any details about a cell phone. They suggested that she was probably using a pay-as-you-go phone, and not in her own name. The checks on her landline were inconclusive. Nearly all of those calls were to the Farmer's Bank in Oldtown; obviously it was there that she had got the finance for her new house. "But," said Eddie, as they discussed their findings later that day, "while we are moving slowly forward I'm not sure where it is leading us. As I repeatedly said, we need a break."

Chapter 25

On the following Tuesday Shirley headed down to Oldtown; ostensibly to do further research but in fact, it was as a result of an invitation from Kaley Brown to have lunch with herself and Alice.

By the time Shirley got back from Oldtown it was night time. Kaley had insisted on cooking one of her special lunches for both Alice and her. "My immediate task in life is to put some meat back on your bones, Alice Newman." she had proclaimed. "And Shirley Green, I just don't know how to thank you enough for all you have done, you must join us."

Two hours later, after the most scrumptious four course lunch. Shirley had to drag herself away from the warmth of Kaley's hospitality and face the almost two-hour drive north to Oakville. She had phoned Butch to explain where she was and to tell him that she had a great idea for another show. Then she had phoned Eddie to tell him that she had the most fantastic meal with Alice and Kaley and that she probably would not eat again for at least a week!

"We had a great chat, which I will tell you about. In the meantime, Alice seems to be coming out of herself and trusting me. I had better be careful. If she feels that I am probing too much we could lose her."

"So tell me all?" began Eddie when they were seated on the couch watching the latest news: all of which they found depressing.

"First of all, let me say that Alice seems to have been a very complex person even before she was committed." said Shirley. "She has no living family; both her parents, who had separated, had since died so she was really on her own when she met Gregg."

"That was when she came to Oldtown, having answered an advertisement looking for a law clerk in a local law firm, Newman and Stuart," interjected Eddie.

"Yep, from their first meeting they both wanted each other and everything in the garden seemed to smell of roses."

"So when did things start to go wrong?" asked Eddie.

"According to Alice, at first she was in awe of Gregg's newfound friends, The Wolf Pack. They were a very tight group of highly motivated young aspiring business people who played hard and worked hard. A group that set its sights high and apparently aimed for the top. Whatever their current enterprise was they would source the people who could achieve it for them and when they had achieved their objective, they would jettison them like deadwood. It was only later on that she realized this.

Apparently, in Gregg's case they saw the perfect opportunity to get control of the City Hall. He was the ideal candidate for the position. He was tall, strong, handsome and talented and with a respectable pedigree. So they stalked him and sucked him in and then began to groom him for the part. They eventually would own him – lock stock and barrel."

"How many were in The Pack?" enquired Eddie.

"Alice said that originally there were seven but, however one died and was not replaced. At the time Alice and Gregg got married they were all either after transferring to Oakville or were about to. That was where the action was and they were an integral part of it. Notwithstanding that, Alice never knew when or how many of them would just descend on their home and expect her to ply them with drink and food. She was never a part of their discussions. However, from time to time she would eavesdrop until Gregg caught her one evening and hit her. 'That is nothing to what the others will do to you if they ever find you listening,' he had warned her. After that she said that she was more careful."

"Kaley then reiterated what she had earlier told Shirley of her experience in trying to find out where Alice had gone when she had disappeared. For months she made enquiries and constantly phoned Gregg's office in her efforts to find out what had happened to her friend. Finally, she was warned in no uncertain manner to keep away from Gregg and stop pursuing her inquiries regarding Alice's wellbeing. She was never in doubt but that her life had been threatened. Most of the people in The Pack were well known to her. She had watched them push their way upwards at every chance they got. They were the people to know if you wanted anything done. Then one day they upped and went off to take over Oakville. That was the way Kaley saw it." said Shirley.

"A very interesting group." said Shirley.

"I wonder!" said Eddie.

"You wonder what? Eddie, what's bugging you now?"

"Oh nothing much. I just wonder how they became so rich and successful. Which they all appear to be. That's all."

Just as they were about to turn out the lights Eddie's cell phone rang.

"Damn it! Who could be calling at this hour of the night?"

It was a call from Pete Chary, the duty officer at the station.

"Sorry for disturbing you at this hour of the evening Eddie but I can't seem to be able to contact the Chief. His phone is going to answering machine. There has been an accident here on the new building site. It appears that one of the workmen was examining work on the roof and that he slipped off the scaffolding and got impaled on the protective fencing. It looks like he is dead. I have called the emergency services and I think I hear the ambulance coming just now. Again apologies for disturbing you sir. I just needed to report it to someone."

"Thanks Pete, just make sure to secure the site of the accident and advise forensics. I will try and make contact with the Chief on his landline. But what the hell was a workman doing up on the roof at this time of night I wonder?"

At this stage Eddie was pulling on his clothes and turning to Shirley he said, "Sorry honey but I have to go out for a short while. A worker has fallen off the scaffolding at the station and it appears that he is dead. I just need to make sure that we have enough resources to handle it. Keep the bed warm. I won't be long!"

On his way out to his car he called the station. "Hi Pete, did anyone call Suarez? You don't have his number? Just go out and get it from the hoarding, it is plastered all over it. If you can't get him, try the architect or quantity surveyor, their numbers are also on the hoarding."

It was another five minutes before Eddie eventually got in touch with the Chief who had been out socialising with his wife.

"Damn it!" was his initial response. "Any idea who he was and why he was there? Did anyone think to contact the contractor, Jeff Suarez?"

"No, I have no idea who he is or what he was doing on the roof at this time of night." replied Eddie. "I'm on my way down to see that everything is under control and if I think it necessary I will call in a few of our squad just to protect the scene until daylight."

By the time he got the station the ambulance and fire tender were already there and the site was taped off.

"Any idea what happened?" Eddie asked as soon as he entered the station.

"We haven't gone up to examine the scaffolding yet." said Sergeant Teddy Johan, who had taken charge of the situation. "But we did shine a light on it and it would appear that the metal clip holding the crossbar at that point had come loose. He either leaned against it or on it and it gave way. The medics are currently removing the body from the fencing and when they have it down we hope to find out who he is."

"Did anyone see him enter the site?" asked Eddie.

"Yep, I saw him entering the site about an hour or so ago talking on his cell phone. I assumed he was one of the contractors. He was complete with hi-viz jacket and hard hat and had a key to the gate. He seemed to know what he was about." said Chary who had joined Johan, "so we didn't query him."

"So who found him?" asked Eddie.

"I thought I heard a noise and went out to have a look," said Chary. "At first I saw nothing but just as I was about to go back inside I caught the glimpse of a hi-viz jacket hanging on the fence, which wasn't there when I was out thirty minutes earlier. When I went to have a closer look I discovered that it was a body."

Just then one of the medics came in to say that they had now taken the body down and that according to his ID his name was Jeffery Suarez.

"Are you sure?" asked Eddie in disbelief.

"Well, apart from the evidence we found in his wallet, he also had his security card around his neck and the photo definitely confirmed it."

Immediately Eddie called the Chief.

"Chief, I hope you are sitting down. The body has been taken down and according to documentation in his wallet which was confirmed by the security card around his neck, it's Jeff Suarez."

"Oh dear God! Are you sure? Has anyone actually identified him?"

"Well the medics have but none of us here have had access to the body as yet. I am about to do that now, I thought you would want to know immediately. I remember you telling me that he was in the habit of doing spot checks on the building when the workers had left. That would explain what he was doing there. I will have a look before they take him away."

They were about to put the body in a body-bag when Eddie asked to see it. It was only yesterday that he had seen Suarez striding down Columba Avenue full of life. Now the face was contorted in terror having fallen to his death. There was no doubt in Eddie's mind: this was the body of Jeff Suarez.

Immediately the police set their own enquiry into the circumstances surrounding the death. The insurance company concerned and the city council also set up enquiries.

A few days later, after post mortem was completed, the funeral of Jeff Suarez took place in the city center. It was a huge affair. It even made both the evening and late night news on NTTV with Shirley Green covering both the service and the interment. After all, his construction company had built at least sixty per cent of the buildings in Oakville. His sons Ron and Jed, who were in their early thirties, would now have to try and fill their father's shoes; not an easy task.

His close friends Al McNally, Leo Forrest, Teddy Moran and Mark Reilly, The Wolf Pack, had helped them to carry their father's coffin into the church.

As he walked back to his car with Mary Donnelly, feeling partly responsible for the death, the Chief said, "It is as a result of my call to him that he would visit the site at night to put the pressure on the workers to get the finger out. Now he is dead and that puts the completion date back even further."

The finding of the insurance company's investigation, which was held sometime later was Accidental Death due to the faulty installation of part of the scaffolding. This finding was hotly contested by both the scaffolding installation company and the construction company, both of which served notice to contest the finding.

Chapter 26

That evening after the burial had taken place, Don Harding, the owner of the Oldtown Chronicle, took Eddie and Shirley up on their invitation to join them for a meal at their place. He had been making every effort to get his body back in some sort of shape after years of Teddy's Diner fast food and knew that Shirley would understand if he was picky about what he now ate. He had come up from Oldtown not only to pay his respects to the Suarez family but to make sure that his reporter and cameraman got full and comprehensive coverage and photographs of the event. After all Jeff Suarez was an Oldtown boy who had made good.

As they watched the coverage of the funeral on the TV after the meal, Don concluded, "The old saying 'you can't take it with you' is surely true. Only sixty-two years of age, worth a fortune and dead. That's sad."

"But how did he do it? How did he make such a success of his life in such a short time?" asked Eddie.

"Well now there are many versions, depending on who you talk to but if you have time and nothing to do, I'll tell you my version," said Don. "In my opinion it started in the country club. They managed to become members of the club at a very early age and I might add in some cases, without the required pedigree for entrance to that club. They were The Wolf Pack, known to some as The Pack: if Sinatra could have the Rat Pack, Oldtown could have its Wolf Pack."

"Did they all come from Oldtown?" asked Shirley.

"Yes they all grew up in Oldtown before heading up to Charleston College and returning with their various pieces of parchment. Forrest majored in Constitutional Law, Suarez in Engineering, McNally in Company Law, Moran in Economics, Reilly in Family Law and Mackey in Medicine. The seventh guy wasn't there very often and wasn't from Oldtown, I think his name was Ashton."

"Did they set up a partnership of some sort or other? Is that how they worked?" asked Shirley.

"No I don't think so." said Don "It appeared that they just became a semi-private, some would say secret, club with the objective of making loads of dollars for each other. And boy did they succeed?"

"I'm still not sure how it worked." said Eddie.

"Well, again I am only surmising, but supposing one of them in his capacity as attorney, found out that his client was in financial difficulty, that information would be pooled within The Pack and might open up opportunities for some or all of the others to make a killing. Not illegal but definitely not ethical and usually very profitable." said Don.

"But surely that couldn't account for the wealth they accumulated?" said Shirley.

"No, but it gave them seed money. Enough to get started. I think the big change came when Oldtown lost out to Oakville."

"How do you mean lost out?" asked Eddie.

"Pour me another coffee, sit back and I will tell you the story." replied Don.

With a fresh mug of tea in his hand, Don told them the story. Over thirty years previously, as part of the State Development Plan a new additional north south freeway was to be built to the east of the state. This new freeway was to be just three miles to the west of Oldtown. The existing 'Freeway 1' was a hundred miles further to the west. All of a sudden Oldtown began to see a bright future and everyone scrambled to get a piece of the action. Land was bought up and prices soared. Plans for the development of a new Municipal Center were drawn up by a company headed by Jeff Suarez, and submitted for planning approval. The sky was the limit, at least it was until it fell in on Oldtown with a bang.

"What happened?" asked Shirley.

"Well," replied Don, "the guy who mapped out the

original route didn't do a proper job of it and another geologist did a subsequent report that stated that the proposed route, as per the plans, was over some fault-line and was not safe. It would need to be moved two miles further east. This apparently caused panic in the Governor's office as by that stage the construction of the freeway was well underway. The guy who had drawn up the plan was fired and a new route was very quickly decided on bringing the freeway to just one mile west of Oldtown - effectively squeezing the town between the lake and the freeway. Now Oldtown had no room to expand but Oakville did."

"That must have caused panic," suggested Eddie.

"It sure did," said Don.

Don then went on to say that a lot of people had to be compensated. One of them being the construction company headed by Suarez. Not only did he get compensation for the land that he had to surrender to enable the freeway to pass by, but he was given the concession, complete with planning permission, to relocate his planned Municipal Center to Oakville. This, as you know, is now one of the finest in the state. So Oldtown shrank while Oakville blossomed and took the best brains with it, leaving the likes of Don to live on the scraps.

"So that's how it was done? Just by moving a line on a map. The freeway did the rest," said Eddie. "Were you ever tempted to go?"

"No, I'm afraid I am not the moving kind. Oldtown is my town," said Don. "I was born there and grew up there and hopefully I will die there. I was never one for chasing the rainbow or for thinking that the grass was greener anywhere else." Pausing and looking pensive he continued. "I wonder what Suarez is thinking now? That is if a person's mind doesn't die when their body dies. Was it worth his time chasing the rainbow?"

"I must admit I like Oldtown." said Shirley, "The people there are oh so friendly and everything about it is laid-back and charming. None of the frenetic running and racing we get here in Oakville." Turning to Eddie she said mischievously, "Hey Eddie, will we up sticks and move to Oakville? I'm sure Don would find us a nice little bungalow that would need a little fixing up. You could grow vegetables and I would get a Doris Day gingham apron and cook all day while singing Oh what a beautiful morning!"

"Maybe I could direct traffic in the square!" replied Eddie sarcastically.

"I think it is time I went to bed," said Don. "This conversation is getting far too intellectual for my poor brain. Is this what eventually happens to everybody who lives in a city?"

Chapter 27

Next morning, after breakfast, as Don was getting ready to return to Oldtown, Shirley said, "Don't stray too far from us Don; you are one of the good guys. Also I need to talk to you a lot more about the demise of Oldtown. I am trying to get Butch to do a series on various aspects of our glorious state and where better to start than in Oldtown, it has such a fascinating history."

"Sure, that sounds like fun but remember a lot of what I told you last evening is hearsay. You don't mess around with some of the people I mentioned. Be careful."

When Don had left and Eddie had gone to work, Shirley sat down and started making notes on a pad. The first page she headed, The Wolf Pack and listed the seven names that Don had mentioned. She then googled each of them, making notes as she read about them. The second page she headed: Oldtown - winners and losers.

To find the winners and losers she needed information. As far as she could see that question had to be divided into those who actually lost money and those who lost 'possible' money. So, she said to herself, my first task is to get the records of all land sales for Oldtown for the period in question. Then see if any of The Pack featured in the records. So her next stop would be to the land registry office which was up in the capital. I think it is time to talk to Butch, she said to herself. This could be big and I need his blessing if I am going to spend a lot of time on it.

"Hi Shirley," said Butch when she entered his office, "you did a good job on the filming of the funeral yesterday; now I need you to edit it. It's forty-five minutes long and I need it cut down to ten at the most. Look through it and pick out the important bits and tie them in with the people of interest who were there. A few other stations want copies. By the way – I need it by three p.m."

"Ok, but when I finish the job, I need to talk to you. I have an idea for you to chew on." she replied with a satisfied grin on her face.

It wasn't long before that Butch was giving her the jobs that nobody else wanted. Now she had just been asked to edit a program all on her own! Could life get any better? The only down side was that she would have to cancel lunch with Eddie, that she regretted.

"Hi honey, bad and good news! Which do you want to hear first?" said Shirley when she eventually got to talk to Eddie.

"Give me the bad first then I will at least have the good taste in my mouth to finish!"

"Ok, the bad news is I have to cancel lunch. I have a

deadline of three p.m. and to have any chance of making it will mean scrapping lunch. Sorry a ton. The good news is that Butch has given me the job of editing the coverage of Suarez's funeral. Now that's progress, don't you think?"

"Wow, that's fantastic. Well done! Tell Butch I will forgive him this time but not to make a habit of it, I hate eating on my own!"

By two thirty Shirley had the job done and was sitting beside Butch as he ran through the edited tape.

"Good. Good. I see you got all of Suarez's family looking dignified and sad. That looks good. You also got his buddies in very interesting groups. It's amazing what the camera picks up when people don't realize they are being filmed."

"I tried to get the dignitaries with the family and The Pack with their connections and finally I picked out some 'ordinary' citizen groupings just to give local flavor. I thought that some of his old classmates and neighbors who were present might like to see that they were recognized for being there."

"Yes I noticed that, good thinking. I will make a TV reporter out of you yet!"

"And then you will have to pay me a decent wage."

Just as they were reaching to end of the tape, Butch

paused and went back a few frames.

"Any idea who that is in that group?" Butch asked as he squinted at a shot of four people, three men and a woman.

"No I don't," said Shirley, "but the reason I included them in was because there seemed to be something different about them. Initially I thought that they were all separate but later I thought maybe not. The woman looks vaguely familiar, but to be honest I don't know any of them. Do you want me to take that piece out?"

"No, it's good. Well done, just leave it as it is."

"Now I want to put my idea for a new program to you," said Shirley.

"Why do I feel I am being set up?" asked Butch as he looked sideways at Shirley.

"Now, what makes you think that? On second thoughts, don't answer that! Last evening Eddie and I were having dinner with Don. The chat got around to talking about Oldtown and how it lost out to Oakville. It was a fascinating story, which I'm sure you know well. Anyway, I was thinking of doing a kind of general historical program on exactly what went on. How the plan changed and who were the winners and who were the losers. I'm sure a lot of people would love to know the inside story. What do you think?"

"What do I think?" mused Butch, "I think it would be dynamite. If we could get away with it. All I can say is that there are a lot of powerful people who wouldn't like it one tiny little bit. But that never stopped us before. What have you in mind?"

"The first thing I need to do is find out is what land was sold in Oldtown. Both in the area stretching out to where the freeway was originally planned to be and at the time of the change in the plan. Then I would need to check the purchases back to those who were compensated and what they did with the land they had purchased. I would be paying special attention to our Wolf Pack."

"Shirley I don't think you realize the type of people you are dealing with. Be careful. Be very careful. Go ahead with it but go slowly and I want you to keep me posted on a daily basis, on precisely what you are doing. Have no doubt that I will pull the plug on the first sign of trouble. Is that clear?"

"Yes sir, it's as clear as could be."

If Shirley had realized what a minefield she was entering, she would never have made her suggestion to Butch. No one had ever told her that the transfer of land was nothing like buying or selling a car. Her biggest surprise was the practice of taking options on large tracts of land with just small deposits being paid. To add to that, a considerable number of offers to buy were made by nominee companies with registered offices outside of the jurisdiction.

After days of slogging through the records she was little the wiser as to who bought what and when. However, what she did discover was that only one who actually bought and paid for land was Suarez. And he had bought vast tracts of it. When she then looked at the compensation claims she discovered that these tracts matched exactly with the proposed planning application that Jeff Suarez had submitted.

As most of the other sales were for very small units of land and had never gone beyond paying a small deposit, she concluded that in all probability these were small investors taking a gamble. She now had a list of their names and would eventually include interviews with them in the series if she thought that it would add value. The big fish she was looking for was Suarez. He was the main player. Who in turn was linked to The Wolf Pack. Very interesting.

"You're skating on very thin ice, Shirley," was Butch's reaction when Shirley had gone over her findings with him. "Our legal boys would never let us air a single piece of that. There is nothing illegal in what you have. Not one thing to show that a crime has been committed. But don't give up, you are on to something and I smell it too! I smell something rotten and I smell a good story."

"'Thank you." said Shirley, feeling very pleased with herself.

"Oh and by the way, remember that still shot from the funeral review you did a few weeks ago? Well I remember where I saw that lady before. She is connected to the Minerva Clinic. I knew the face was familiar but can't remember her name."

"Any idea who the others in the frame are?" Shirley asked.

"No idea. Did you say that you thought they knew each other?"

"No. But I got the impression that they were together, but not together, if you know what I mean. It was like they didn't want people to think that they knew each other. Oh God did I just say that? Now I know I am cracking up. That sounds like the wanderings of a demented mind. Forget I ever mentioned it!"

"Lack of food does that you know. You probably don't realize that it is now three p.m. and you haven't eaten, so pack you bag and go home and take your fiancé out for a nice dinner on NTTV. You're doing well. Tomorrow is another day and may I suggest that you start it by applying the same investigative procedure that you used on Oldtown to Oakville. That might give us something we can use. Also I might mention that your Chat with Shirley program has been getting much positive comment. I am thinking of making it a weekly show. I will talk to you later when I have thought it through. Now off with you and enjoy a good meal."

That evening as she dined out with Eddie in a new upmarket Italian restaurant, at NTTV's expense, they were comparing notes on their day. Shirley was gushing about her exciting day and how Butch was now mentoring her for a weekly show. Six months earlier he was sending her out to watch vegetables grow.

"I'm so happy for you, honey. It is well overdue, you are really good at what you do and you have a great work ethic."

"Thanks Eddie, I am learning so much from you. Before I met you I would just barge in with my idea, thinking that it was the best. Then I would take it personally if it was rejected – which it was, or nearly always was. Now here I am again going on and on, when I notice that you haven't said one word about your day. Tell me all."

"The problem is that there is very little to tell. Nothing seems to be moving on any of my main cases. Just when I think we are getting a breakthrough, the door closes and we are back to scratch."

"That must be very frustrating but I know my Eddie, and you won't give up. That reminds me, do you remember me telling you about the job of editing that I did a few weeks ago? Well it's amazing who the camera sees and records."

"I'm sure it must be. Many a man regretted picking his nose or texting someone without realizing that the image is gone out on the airways across the state."

"Yes indeed, but there was one interesting group that I had focused in on as the mourners left the church. It was just a random casual shot of three gentlemen and one woman. Don't ask me what made them interesting to me at the time as I didn't know any of them. However Butch did, and here is the connection: the lady is in some way connected to the Minerva Clinic. Butch couldn't remember her name unfortunately."

"Are you sure? Describe her to me." said an enlivened Detective Eddie McGrane.

When Shirley described her as best she could, Eddie said, "From the picture you have painted it looks like our friend Jane Starling. Not only is she turning up in the most unlikely places with strangers that she 'doesn't seem to know,' but she also seems to be changing her appearance like a chameleon. I wonder what she was doing at that funeral."

Chapter 28

When Eddie got into work the following morning there was a note on his desk to say that Doctor Moody had called three times the previous evening. There was also a note to say that a Jane Starling had called and left a number at which she could be contacted. Before he had got around to calling either of them back, his phone rang again.

"Hello detective, Quintin Moody here calling from Wayward Creek. Do you remember me?"

"Of course I do," replied Eddie, "wasn't I talking to you only yesterday? How could I forget all the good work you have done for us. So how are you today?"

"Today is a good day; all my parts seem to be working and that is not always the case. However, I have news for you, Detective."

"Delighted to hear that, Doctor. What's your news?"

"Well I have discovered that your friend up here, the one you were enquiring about, has a lover! It appears that the Haven Clinic, where she works, employed a rather handsome driver a few months ago and apparently cupid shot his arrow at both. I am told, the romance is blossoming. I hope that fills in a few of your blank spaces."

Having thanked him for his efforts and asking him

to keep his eyes open for any change in the relationship, Eddie finished the call. "She's a strange one." he said to himself. "Not a good month so far. I will have to go back to the beginning, back to Alice. I still believe that she has the key to it all if only she realized it."

He then returned Jane Starling's phone call.

"Sorry I missed your call, Ms Starling. What can I do for you?"

"I have spoken with my attorney regarding the question of my finger prints and he has allayed my fears. He said that there was no question of my prints ending up being stored in some big terrorist file and kept forever."

"I can assure you that was never on the cards."

"Well, as a matter of fact I am presently here in Oakville and will be returning to Wayward Creek tomorrow afternoon. If it suited, you I could call into the station in the morning. I assume it doesn't take long to do the job."

"Fifteen minutes max. By the way, as you may know already, while the station is being reconstructed, our unit is located in the street opposite the station, Number 1115 on the left hand side. Can you make it for eleven thirty?"

"No problem, see you then."

As soon as he ended the call he rang Tom Bradshaw.

"Hi Mr Bradshaw, Detective Eddie McGrane here," began Eddie as he was put through. "Listen, I have a few questions I would like to put to your client, Alice Newman. I wonder if you could arrange for us to meet, in your presence of course."

"Leave it with me and I will get back to you as soon as I have spoken to her."

Chapter 29

Next day, at precisely eleven thirty, Starling entered the office. At first glance Eddie didn't recognize her and it wasn't just Botox. It was the way that she walked and held herself that had been transformed. Added to that was her new hair style and make-up. It had transformed her appearance. She actually looked happy for a change. Gone was the servile attitude, the thick grey stockings, and the horn framed spectacles and of course the long grey hair, which had usually been tied back by an elastic band. Today she wore a beige tweed coat over a stylish designer navy suit. Her hair was styled to shoulder length and colored auburn. Her face was lightly made up, not overdone but just enough to give her face a more pleasant look. However, her eyes were still cold and distant.

"Thank you so much for coming in today, it saves us a lot of time, not having to drive all the way up to Wayward Creek. We appreciate that."

While Maria was setting up the fingerprinting unit, Eddie was making small talk.

"So how are you settling in to your new environment?"

"So far so good." she said. "The staff are excellent and while we have slightly fewer patients, we are kept very busy. I like that."

"I assume they have provided you with accommodation in the clinic, or at least until you find a place of your own?" said Eddie - probing for information

"Oh God no! I wouldn't put up with that. No, a friend of mine has a small place and we share it. It's very near the clinic which is ideal."

"What luck? Did you know about the house before you took the job?"

"No I didn't, as a matter of fact it all came together very suddenly shortly after I got there."

'Lies.' thought Eddie.

"That must have made the transition from Oakville easier for you. But I'm sure you miss Oakville, do you come back often?"

"Yes, it did ease the way for me. To be quite honest I don't miss Oakville at all. Other than to visit some of the boutiques I have little reason to come up. The only reason I am here today is in connection with the death of Jeff Suarez. A friend had some business connection with the Suarez Company. It was a great shock to so many people."

"All very plausible!" said Eddie when Maria had finished taking the fingerprints and Starling had left with a confident stride. Job done.

"We have nothing on her," said Maria. "The

fingerprints on the literature can easily be explained by the fact that she would have every reason to be in Alice's room and handle anything on the table. Remember Matron telling us that she had specifically asked her to befriend Alice."

"I know that but at the moment she is the only game in town and I'm not prepared to throw in the towel yet. Now that we see how she has changed her appearance maybe, just maybe, the woman in the CCTV tape could be her."

"Maybe and maybe not," said Maria, pushing back her chair. "So far no one has been able to identify her."

"One other thing, and I realize that this is a long shot. If…. if she was involved, is it possible that she put the note in the car, and then drove her own car drove to the mall to keep an eye on Alice? If so, her car would be scanned at the barrier, just like Mitchum's car was. Now isn't that an idea?" said Eddie. "Maria would you get one of the extra squad we have to contact the clinic and get the number of Starling's car. Then have them go back and check the scanned numbers at each side of the time Alice entered and left the mall parking. We just might get lucky."

"In the meantime, let's see if we can put a name on her 'friend'. Moody might be able to suss it out from the people at the clinic." Eddie added.

Not wasting any time, Eddie immediately called Moody.

"Hi Doctor Moody, it's me again, your detective friend Eddie. Your information regarding Ms Starling has been corroborated by the lady herself just twenty minutes ago. Yes, she is here in Oakville with a friend! Is it possible for you to find out more of what she is doing up there? For instance, who are her friends? Any information like that would help us."

"Of course. I will do my best, Detective." said Moody.

"She also mentioned to us that she is sharing a small house with a friend who owns it. I'm looking for that friend's name. Who he is and is he the driver you told us about. Thank you Doctor, you have been most helpful."

"Hi Eddie, Bradshaw on line two for you!" shouted the duty officer as Eddie just hung up the phone.

"Good afternoon Tom." They were now on first term names, when it suited. "Hope you have good news for me. I am not having a good day myself. As a matter of fact, I don't think it can get any worse."

"Good news, Alice will see you, but you will have to go to Oldtown. The lady is not for travelling. She is available this afternoon or this day week."

"I'm not going to wait another week just looking across the road watching the buildings slow progression. What time suits you?"

"Well, by a coincidence I'm here in Oldtown. How

long would it take you to get here?"

"Two hours if my partner is driving and one hour thirty if I am. Why don't we say two thirty at the Colonial Hotel on Main Street?"

"Perfect, see you then."

Looking at his watch he estimated that he had a little over three hours to get there, enough time to grab lunch at the local diner, coffee and a hot-dog.

When Maria and Eddie got to the hotel they found that Bradshaw had positioned himself and Alice at a corner table at the end of the reception area. Bradshaw looked his usual frazzled self while Alice looked graceful and serene.

"Good afternoon Ms Newman, I really appreciate you taking the time to see me," said Eddie as he shook hands with her. "Good to see you too Mr Bradshaw."

Having dispensed with pleasantries, Bradshaw asked, "How can we help you, Detective?"

"We have been looking back over the interview we had with you shortly after your release from the clinic and there are one or two things we would like to ask you about again, if you please." said Eddie.

"May I remind you once again, Detective, that my client may refuse to answer any question that I feel might implicate her in any wrong-doing."

"Yes, we appreciate that and we do not intend any breach of her rights. Now if I may, I would like to ask you about your relationship with the staff of Minerva, excluding Doctor Mitchum."

"I'm not sure what you mean Detective. Of course I interacted with those nurses who medicated me in as much as I could. Likewise, I interacted with the people who fed me. Is that what you want?"

"No, not really. I am trying not to direct you in any one direction. I want to hear how you answer the question. Let me put it more directly by giving you an example. How did you relate to Matron Smyth?"

"Matron Smyth? I had little or no communication with her."

"Ok, now how about assistant matron Starling?"

"Well, initially I don't recall having anything to do with her but in the last year or there about she seemed to have taken a particular interest in me. I assumed that Doctor Mitchum had asked her to look after me as a special project."

"In what way exactly?" asked Maria.

"She used to visit me sometimes in the evenings and would read the newspapers for me. She was, I felt, checking up on my eating habits, to make sure I wasn't suffering from bulimia or some such disorder. For many years, that is until Doctor Mitchum took me in hand, I had been losing a lot of weight."

"I'm sure her concern was for your health's sake," said Maria. "Did she ever talk about herself? Where she came from, was she ever married, any boyfriends? You know personal chit-chat."

"No, she was a kind of drab person. I'm sorry! I shouldn't have used that word. What I mean is that she appeared to lack energy. I just couldn't see her as someone's girlfriend, let alone wife. Her whole life seemed to be looking after someone like me."

"I want you to think carefully about the next question, Ms Newman. Do you think that assistant matron Starling knew that Doctor Mitchum allowed you to use his car and leave the clinic?" asked Eddie.

Turning to Bradshaw, she asked, "Is it alright to answer that question?"

"Yes, I don't see any reason why not."

"While I am not sure, I think she did. But if she did, she never squealed on me. It was just something she said to me one evening as we were talking while I was preparing for bed. Out of the blue she just said, 'can you drive?' I was flummoxed. What a question to ask? That very day I had driven to our house just to get a glimpse of my daughter. What a shock I got. Of course I denied ever having driven and she just left it at that."

"Can you think of any other person who would have known that you would be borrowing the car on that day?"

"No, absolutely not. We, Doctor Mitchum and I, we were so careful. His job depended on absolute secrecy."

"Very good, now one final question," said Eddie. "On the day that Doctor Mitchum died, you had driven to the mall and parked the car in the basement car park. Can you remember anything about that whole event? Other than the note you found in the car. Was there anything strange or anybody out of place in the basement that you can recall?"

"No, and even if there was I don't think I would have noticed. Initially I was so excited at the prospect of seeing my daughter and then when she didn't turn up I was so stressed out realizing that I had kept the doctor waiting. My driving, if I recall, was erratic. I was in such a hurry."

"Thank you so much, Ms Newman," and turning to Bradshaw he continued, "and to you for facilitating our request. We very much appreciate your time and effort. Now we must head back to base but if you think of anything else, please call either Detective Diego or myself at any time – day or night."

On the drive back to Oakville, Eddie asked Maria, "Well what did you make of that?"

"Well Eddie, we know that someone knew that she would be taking the car on that day. That someone put a note in the car – that's a fact. Now according to Alice, Starling had gotten very close and personal with her and would visit her in the evenings just as she would be preparing for bed; a time when she would have had her night-time medication. In other words, she would have been vulnerable and open to questioning. I believe Starling has a lot to answer. What do you think?"

"I couldn't agree with you more. Yes, I think she knew and yes, I think she put the note in the car. But who asked her to do it? We need to have a very close look at Ms Starling. Up to now she has basically been invisible; she just blended in with the wood-work, so to speak."

Chapter 30

For the next few days Shirley was busy checking out the record of land sales and purchases in and around Oakville. What she discovered was interesting. It appeared that in the twelve-month period prior to the freeway changing direction, approximately six square miles of land adjoining Oakville had been purchased by Jeff Suarez who was obviously putting together a portfolio of land. Apparently it involved the purchase of twenty-two separate units of land. Some arable, some brush land and some working farms. The total purchase price was four million dollars. All payments were made through the Farmers Bank in Oldtown. On further investigation she discovered that Jeff Suarez had sold various parcels of land to a large number of individuals and among that number was each member of The Wolf Pack.

Her next move was to check up on the Suarez Construction Company and see from whom they had purchased the land on which they had built the Municipal Center on. Once again the paper trail was convoluted. It appeared that Jeff Suarez had sold two square miles of the land to the Suarez Construction Company. However, she could not find a record of Suarez receiving any payment from any of the sales.

"Once again I can see no obvious crime here," said Butch when she was going over her findings with him. "If it was only The Wolf Pack who bought land we might have some reason to question it. However, he bought the full store and the buyers queued up to buy the goodies – so to speak."

"OK so what you are saying is that a company bought land in anticipation of a demand; call it a gamble or whatever. Then having commandeered ownership of the available land, it became a seller's market. And there is nothing wrong with that – but where did he get the money to buy land both in Oldtown and in Oakville?" asked Shirley.

"A very good question, Shirley, but remember it is only a short time since Jeff Suarez died. We need to be extra careful not to offend his family or indeed his many friends in Oakville. I can see no obvious illegality here."

"How about we do a program on Oldtown pointing out the benefits from not becoming the second city. We could get Don to give a brief history of the place and show the unique, peaceful and picturesque town that it is. That would give it a huge boost, the town really needs it. Someone has to invest in its potential. After all it is only two hours from Oakville and could easily become a satellite town to Oakville." pleaded Shirley.

"Ok. Put it together and let me see what you've got and I will then decide. But keep it short and snappy, thirty minutes only. Ok?"

The next day Shirley booked in to the Colonial Hotel having graciously turned down Kaley Brown's offer of accommodation. She knew that if she accepted the offer she would have difficulty concentrating on the job in hand, too many offers of a chat and apple pie. Now she would be able to entertain both Kaley and Alice to meals at the hotel and then get some work done. Six days later having worked out of a spare office in the Oldtown Chronicle office, she had the skeleton of the program ready for Butch.

"You don't give up easily, do you? But how you have managed to insert your suspicions regarding The Wolf Pack into a seemingly innocuous travelogue extolling the virtues of Oldtown's simple and attractive country lifestyle. I don't know! You even got the likes of retired Judge Leo Forrest and Teddy Moran, Chairman of the local bank to give you their opinion on film." said Butch.

"You always said that in order to give credence to any report you needed to have the report substantiated by quotes from persons of note in the community," she said with a grin. "We had Forrest on our last program and apart from showing that he is a good performer in front of the cameras, he is a local Oldtown boy who did well. As for Moran, well it's in his interest to promote Oldtown and knowing as we do, that his bank was up to its eyes in the financing of the land deals. Who knows he just might let his guard slip."

"Shirley Green, you are devious! Let me run it past our legal watchdogs and see what they say. Personally I think it is good and interesting and dynamite! I think it would make a good follow-up to your first three Chat with Shirley programs!"

A week later the program finally went on air.

Setting the opening scene was an overview of the town and surrounding area, taken by a drone. It showed the town and the lakes, both lower and upper, and the freeway as it wound its way northwards to Oakville. As the camera seemed to rise out of the ground and fly northwards it showed clearly the course of the freeway to the west and the lower lake to the east. All along the lake shore were sport shops and activity centers, offering everything and anything to do with water sports. As the camera headed northwards over the pine covered hills that separated the lakes, it showed the upper and the bigger of the two lakes with the ever expanding Oakville at its northern tip.

The program then switched to the studio panel and introducing each one giving some background information on them. Then, before engaging the panel in the discussion, individual interviews were conducted with local people in their own work environment. First to be interviewed was Don Harding from the Chronicle. He was interviewed on the street outside of his office. To try and fit a camera crew together with Don and Shirley inside his upstairs office would not be good TV coverage. As a local who knew the area well and claimed to have his finger on the pulse of the town, he covered the background of the arrival of the freeway and its consequences for the town. Naturally he put a positive spin on it, claiming that it actually made Oldtown a better and more sought after place to live in.

Then the camera wandered around the streets picking out various buildings such as the brightly painted quaint little shops that sold everything from Christmas cards to drums of heating oil and sweets of all shapes and sizes. The camera then zoomed in on the equally quaint diners, bars and ice-cream parlours, bringing the viewers on a trip around the narrow streets of Oldtown, always picking out the best looking buildings and ending up at the war memorial in the town's square. There Don gave an emotional commentary: emotional because it commemorated all those who died fighting in World War Two, his own brother being among them.

The camera then reverted to the studio where the long serving Chief of Police Bart Mellows, a man in his early sixties, six feet two tall and carrying one hundred and eighty-five pounds' weight and with a deceptively easy going manner, was sitting beside Teddy Moran, Chairman of the local Farmers Bank and who was beginning to look the worse for wear. Moran never did like facing the cameras and had always, if possible, avoided being photographed. When Shirley asked him to tell her how and when he had started work in the bank he had, he said, commenced work in the bank as a clerk over forty years ago. Over that period, he had worked his way up to manager and then general manager before becoming chairman. Now his five foot two overweight body looked comically pear-shaped. On this occasion he seemed to be in awe of Shirley; maybe he was in fear of the questions Shirley might ask. Beside Moran was retired Judge Leo Forrest, keeping a safe distance between himself and Moran whom he purported to know only as someone from the past.

Shirley played the role of ringmaster, a job she was obviously born to do. She soon had the panel revealing personal details of their reaction to the arrival of the new freeway which she expertly linked by referring back to

Don's earlier walkabout commentary. Throughout the initial discussions, Bart Mellows was just an observer; in typical policeman's style, observe and listen. However, when Forrest commented that it was always inevitable that Oakville would become the second City and Moran appeared to agree with him. Mellows held up both hands and said, "Whoa there boys! Now where did you get that notion? Did you smart boys know something that we didn't?" as he looked from one to the other.

"No, no," replied a somewhat flustered Forrest. "What I meant was that once the decision was taken to reroute the freeway, then the decision in relation to Oakville was obvious and inevitable. That's what I meant."

"Well," said Mellows, "I don't think it was inevitable. If there hadn't been such a panic and God damn hurry at the time... Well maybe there could have been another possibility. However, here we are in this beautiful town and I wouldn't ask to move away from it."

Thirty minutes was not half long enough for Shirley. However, as the drone camera, in its final shot, focused in on Oldtown like a hawk dropping from the sky on its prey, her closing comment was; "You have seen the TV coverage, now experience the real thing. Visit Oldtown. From Shirley Green for NTTV. Good night and take good care now."

Just as she was about to leave the studio a call came through for her. Another satisfied viewer no doubt.

"Shirley Green?" said the voice on the phone.

"Yes?" said Shirley, hoping that whoever it was wouldn't delay her. She was due to meet up with Eddie.

"You did well tonight," said the voice, "but you missed the obvious. Didn't you?"

"The obvious? What do you mean?"

"The elephant in the room of course. Why is nobody asking why the guy who did the defining geological review? The one that put the cat among the pigeons, so to speak. Why did he die by suicide?"

With that the phone line went dead.

Chapter 31

"What the hell is that all about," Shirley muttered to herself as she stared at the silent phone in her hand. Then, out of the corner of her eye she saw Bart Mellows going out the door. She ran after him, catching up with him just as he was about to get into his car.

"Excuse me, Chief, but can I ask you a question? You see I have just had an unusual phone call. Someone, a male, just called and wanted to know why we weren't discussing the guy who wrote the report that said the original route for the freeway was unsafe. He also said that the guy had died by suicide. Is any of this true?"

"Well now, I can't rightly say young lady. You see hindsight is perfect sight, as my Mom used to say. Here we are now discussing the result of events that were triggered many years ago. What you are now doing is clinically examining and debating the events that brought about the change in direction of the freeway. Now my memory of that time is that it was of little consequence to most folks. To some it was seen as a blessing, after all, the through flow of traffic would be passing nearer to Oldtown with the prospect of adding more business opportunities to the town folk. Then you had the movers and shakers who saw something different, possibly lost opportunities. So, what I am saying is that whoever it was who filed that report, and I don't remember knowing who it was, just moved on and to my knowledge he was never heard of again."

"But was he a local?"

"I don't think so. If he was, his name or something about him, would surely have stuck in my memory. Now as regards dying by suicide, well I never heard of it, but then how would I if he had left the state? I think you just got a crank call Shirley, nothing more."

But Shirley wasn't so sure. All the way home she replayed that voice in her mind. It didn't sound like the voice of a crank. It was too measured and quiet and reasonable for that. Above all, the question he had asked made perfect sense.

Why had nobody mentioned it? And, from her own point of view why had she not thought of it? Probably because, as Bart had suggested, it was of little consequence to most people. As soon as she got home she would ask Eddie; he would have a view on it.

As soon as she got home she told Eddie what had happened and what Bart Mellows had said.

"Well first of all let me congratulate you on another brilliant show," began Eddie. "That's four shows in four months. When is Butch going to make it a weekly show?

Or at the very least a fortnightly show. The ratings are there to prove that you are a winner. The advertisers must be knocking at his door."

"Thanks honey, you are biased but you do give a girl a morale boost! Now regarding the future of the show, well Butch has mentioned the possibility of making it a weekly show. I didn't want to mention it just yet as Butch has a nasty habit of changing his mind quite suddenly." she paused and looked him in the eye, "What about the phone call? What do you make of it?"

"I agree with Bart, it obviously didn't cause much of a stir at the time and it is now history. Of course, if you want to find out more about it why not get a copy of the report. It must be filed somewhere. Or, if you are really concerned why not phone the guy back? The station must have a record of his phone call."

"Maybe I am just being paranoid, Eddie or tired, or maybe as you always say – I have an itch and it won't go away. There is something here that needs to be scratched. So first thing in the morning I am going to check out the phone call and then get my hands on the report. The city council must have a record of it. God help me if I have to go up to the state offices, that could mean a long wait while someone gets off of their butt and replies to my request."

"Good idea, but can I remind you Miss Investigator

that tomorrow is Saturday and believe it or not but most offices close for the weekend."

"Then I will have to wait until Monday, won't I?"

Shirley, not being one to give up easily, spent most of Monday waiting for her calls to be answered. She began to wonder if there were any humans left to answer phones. Now it was a question of which option to take, option one two, three, four or even more, while being assured that her call was valued. However, by five p.m. she had the information she was looking for.

"Well Eddie, I finally got an answer to my questions," she began as soon as she got back to the apartment and had shed her shoes. "The name of the guy who did the report was a geologist named Joseph Herbert Ashton, with about fifteen letters after his name. I googled him and found out that he was a very highly thought of person in the area of geological studies. Much sought after all over the US to give lectures on specific issues relating to the strata of the earth and that kind of stuff."

"Was he from around here?" Eddie asked as he pulled two beers from the fridge and handed one to Shirley.

"No, he came from Cedarwood, where I discovered that he was a respected member of the local community. People there told me that he was a quiet and happy kind of guy and a very modest one. Locally they were very proud of his achievements. The entire community was shocked to hear of his death by suicide. He was only fifty-six when he died leaving a wife and three kids, a girl and two boys."

"Did you get talking to the wife?" asked Eddie.

"No, she died a few years ago and no one seemed to know where the kids went. They would be in their thirties now. Apparently, when their mother died they sold the home and went their own ways. One person did hint that one of the sons went wrong or something like that. Just a hint and no more."

"I know that the phone call you got about why the program didn't explore this guy and his suicide is still niggling you. Why don't you do a search in the births and deaths records and get the names of the kids. You may be able to locate one of them and get the inside story. When you have that, Butch may be more amenable to you doing a follow up program that would take in the development of Oakville as the second city."

"That's a great idea and yes, there was something sinister in that phone call. I can't put my finger on what exactly it was but neither can I get it out of my head."

"It was a pity he didn't leave a contact number or even agree to talk to you again. What he said was very vague. He could have been just expressing an annoyance that a part of the program, that meant something personal to him, was being ignored. Hopefully he will follow it up if he doesn't see you reacting. In the meantime, I will see if we can trace the call and if he does call again, try and keep him talking, he might just give something away."

Chapter 32

It was a beautiful Saturday morning and Detective Eddie McGrane was just tying up his sneakers prior to commencing his usual five mile run along the lake shore when his cell phone buzzed.

"Damn it, not on a Saturday morning," said Eddie, before he saw that it was his Chief calling.

"Hi Eddie I know I am interrupting you on a Saturday morning, and I did tell you yesterday to take a few days off, but we have another incident. I need you on it immediately."

"What's up?"

"From initial reports just in, it appears that our old friend Leo Forrest died by suicide at his home this morning. I would like you to round up your partner and get out there and have a look."

"Christ, I think that crowd is out to haunt me. Who's on the case?"

"The local cops and Lennie from forensics are there and also John Crow the pathologist is on his way. You know the house; it is adjacent to the yacht club?"

Thirty minutes later, having changed out of his running gear and having explained to Shirley who was still tucked up in bed, what was happening, he was entering Leo Forrest's home.

Leo Forrest was a big man. Six feet six inches tall and weighing three hundred and fifty pounds. In keeping with its owner, everything in the room was large – everything that is except the small bullet hole in his right temple and the small, pearl-handled .22 calibre pistol in his hand. Not the type of gun one would expect such a big man to have. More like what a lady might have in her handbag. But then Leo was always unpredictable. Now it looked like he was holding a small toy in his hand as he lay sprawled across his desk.

While the Forensic team were checking out the room and awaiting the arrival of the city pathologist, Eddie and his partner Maria, waited in the adjoining reception room. That room, together with the study, with its floor-to-ceiling plate glass windows, took up the entire eastern side of the house with a panoramic view of the lake. To the left hand side was a clear view of the Oakville Yacht Club and Marino and on the right the city of Oakville could be seen coming into view.

Above the granite fireplace hung a painting of retired Judge Leo Forrest, and, as of now, ex-commodore of the Oakville Yacht Club. Three couches and four armchairs, and a number of tea-tables were casually placed around the room. The couches and armchairs looked like, and most likely were genuine leather. A pool table was situated beside a minibar at the far end of the room. No expense had been spared in making it a comfortable gentleman's room.

Leo had obviously known the best place to build his house and had the money to do it well. The magnificent house nestled on the side of the hill, looking down over manicured lawns, onto the lake, where yachts, in a stiff westerly wind, scurried in and out of the marina, practising for the various competitions of the Oakville Yacht Club Regatta which were to be held later today.

"Hi Eddie," said Lennie, from forensics, as he exited the study. "We're finished in here. The doctor is on his way up, I believe."

"Thanks Len. What do you make of it?"

"Looks like he had enough of this life and plugged himself. He didn't even finish his cigar, poor bastard, left half of it in the ashtray and he spilled what looks like the best of brandy on the desk. What a waste!"

"Any idea when he did it?"

"The doctor will tell us more precisely, but I would think that judging from the condition of the wound, he did it last night."

"So who discovered the body?" asked Eddie, as he

continued to take notes in his well-worn notebook.

"It appears that his wife, Nancy, had to go upstate. Apparently her mother had a fall and ended up with a broken hip and was taken to hospital. So Leo was home alone. When he didn't show up for the first race this morning, Mel Govern, the assistant commodore, having failed to get him on the phone, called up to the house but got no response to ringing the doorbell. Then he contacted their son, Richard, who lives in the city. When he arrived fifteen minutes later they entered the house and found him slumped across his desk. He immediately rang the police."

"I didn't know he had a son, never heard much talk about him." Eddie remarked.

"Yeah, I got the feeling there was a distinct gap between father and son, something about independence, you know the way these things are. I heard he was into theatre or acting – something like that. I remember hearing way back that Leo didn't want a son of his involved with that kind of thing. Not macho enough for big Leo. Anyway I'm off now." said Lennie, as he packed up his gear, "You know where I am if you need me. Why do these things always happen on a Saturday? Our day of rest!"

"Thanks Len, before you go – any idea where we might find Mel Govern right now?"

"My guess would be at the yacht club. Someone has

to oversee the day's events, that is, if they decide to go ahead with it. It wouldn't surprise me if they did."

Just then the assistant city pathologist, Simon Magner, arrived and after introducing himself to Eddie and explaining that John Crow, his boss, was on annual leave, set about examining the body.

"Damn it, why did it have to be Simon?" Eddie whispered to Maria, "I hear that he is always so slow. Word has it that he could spend a week just looking at a body before opening it. This is going to take some time, Maria, so I suggest we spend the time having a look around the house, just to get the feel for it and anyway it isn't often we get to see inside a house like this."

The house had been built approximately twenty-five years previously, at the time when most speculators were putting their money on Oldtown becoming the economic and Municipal Center of the state. However, when the surprise decision was taken to build the north south freeway close to Oldtown was made, Leo was already building his mansion in Oakville. It was an amazing coup for Leo. But then he always seemed to be one step ahead of the opposition, except this time.

Built on a five-acre hill site overlooking the lake, it was built on three levels. The ground level consisted of an outdoor swimming pool, barbeque area and three garages.

From here the immaculately cultivated gardens and lawns swept down to the lake and the jetty where a thirty-foot cabin cruiser was berthed; his yacht being berthed at the marina. Both being nothing more than a display of wealth, judging from how infrequently he used either of them.

The first floor contained the kitchen and dining room towards the rear and the entire front contained the large reception room and study, where Leo's body now lay. Both of which led out to a decked veranda that ran the entire length of the house.

Upstairs were the five bedrooms, all with en-suite facilities, and a small gym leading out to a golf practice bay on a veranda where Leo could practice his golf swing in private. Among other things, Leo had been a more than competent golfer.

"For a house like this, there appears to be a distinct lack of CCTV cameras," noted Maria as they passed from floor to floor. "I have noticed only two on the ground floor - one directed on the driveway and the second on the pool area."

"Yep, some people seem to think that they are invincible and then blame the cops when they have a problem."

"I wonder what level of security he had installed?" mused Maria.

"His wife will be able to fill us in on that when she gets home." said Eddie. "I understand their son, Richard, has gone to the airport to collect her and take her back to his place. She should be there shortly. In the meantime, let's see if we can put a timeframe on events."

"Do you think we have time to visit Mel Govern before Simon is finished with his examination? Govern should be able to help in setting a timeframe for us."

"Yeah, good idea. Simple Simon could take a very long time. In the meantime, Govern should be able to tell us when and with whom Leo left the club last night. Let's go. We can pick up where we leave off here when we return."

Having advised Officer Steve Grey, who was on duty outside the study, of their intentions, they drove out the circular driveway and turned right down to the lake road and then left to the yacht club which was only about a half mile. The entire journey took less than five minutes.

Chapter 33

When they arrived at the club entrance they noticed small groups of what looked like competitors, forming around the club entrance. The news of their commodore's death had obviously reached them. Spread around the lawns in front of the club and along the lakefront were the event tents and fast food catering outlets. The club house itself was a two story building with a granite façade with a viewing deck over a long glass fronted restaurant cum bar. Whoever designed it obviously designed Leo's house as well. They had a similarity that was obvious: you could be led to believe it was in fact an extension of Leo's mansion. Having parked the car, they both headed for the entrance.
"Any idea where we might find Mel Govern?" Eddie asked a couple who were just exiting the club, wearing white sailing jackets with the Oakville Yacht Club crest, green oak leaf set against an orange background, emblazoned on them.

"Yeah mister, you will find him in the committee room upstairs."

As they entered the building they were aware of a general air of disarray and panic around the building. Everyone seemed to be whispering in little groups, not knowing what exactly had happened and not knowing if the regatta would continue. Already some of the junior races had begun but the main three senior events had not; they were scheduled for later.

Finding the committee room proved harder than expected. There were at least six doors on each side of the corridor with no indication on any one of them as to what lay behind them. Just as they reached the end of the corridor they encountered a tall gentleman, wearing white slacks, a blue polo-necked sweater and a very worried looking face. He had just emerged from one of the rooms.

"Excuse me sir, can you tell me where we might find Mel Govern? We were told he was in the committee room but then no one told us where that was," said Eddie.

"And who might you be?" enquired the gentleman.

"I'm Detective Eddie McGrane and this is my partner Detective Maria Diego," said Eddie, flashing his ID.

"Sorry, but one can't be careful enough nowadays. I'm Mel Govern and I suppose you are here in connection with the awful news about our commodore. Let's find a more private place to talk," said Mel as he led them to one of the doors on his right hand side.

"This is my office and at least we won't be disturbed in here. Now can you tell me what happened to Leo?"

"Well Mr Govern, on the contrary, we were hoping

that you might be able to tell us what took place. Maybe you could begin by telling us if you noticed anything different about Mr Forrest lately?"

"Anything different? No, Leo was in the best of form all week. He always thrives on the bustle coming up to regatta week, particularly the last one of the season," said Mel, "He was in his element when organizing the details of the week. This year was looking like it would be a particularly successful one with competitor numbers up by thirty-seven percent for our last big regatta of the season."

"So, tell me, was he here all day yesterday?"

"Yes, during regatta week, Leo would always be here from early morning til late at night, and yesterday was no exception."

"Do you know what time he went home?"

"Yes, in fact I do. We had a seven p.m. dinner arranged for our sponsors and some of our very special supporters and at approximately eleven fifteen p.m. I drove him home. When we got to the house the security lights came on. Other than those lights the house was in complete darkness. Leo had omitted to leave some internal lights on, silly man. Obviously he had forgotten that Nancy would not be home."

"And you didn't notice any change in his behavior?"

"Absolutely not. He was in the best of form, the

dinner had gone off exceptionally well with promises of continued sponsorship and support for development work that Leo had in mind for next season. He invited me in for a nightcap but I declined. I had had a very tiring day and had an early start this morning."

"So at what time did you begin to wonder where he might be this morning?" Maria asked.

"Well, last thing he said when he got home last night was: 'I'll be down at 8.00a.m. So don't start the junior races until I arrive. The forecast for the morning is problematic so I want to warn these juniors of the possibility of adverse wind conditions just before the outward turn. If they don't get that right, there could be big problems for all.'

So when he wasn't here by eight fifteen a.m. I called him thinking he may have slept in, his wife being away and all that. However, I couldn't get a reply so at approximately eight thirty a.m. I called up to the house to see was there a problem."

"Did you notice anything out of the ordinary when you got to the house?" asked Eddie.

"No, everything seemed as normal. Some of the blinds were still drawn which in retrospect was a bit unusual as Leo is usually a very early riser and always has an early morning swim before breakfast."

"So at what stage did you decide to contact his son?"

said Eddie as he continued to make notes in his notepad.

"Well, having rang the bell a number of times I walked around the outside of the house to see if there was any sign of Leo. When I found nothing, I called Richard and asked him to come over with his keys to the house. He arrived after about fifteen minutes. He lives just on the edge of town."

"Did Richard seem surprised that you called him?" asked Eddie.

"Yes, at first he said he was busy and had better things to do on a Saturday morning but eventually when I pleaded with him, he relented. I told him that the success of the regatta depended on us waking Leo up or something like that. I had a way with Richard and always had a soft spot for him; he seemed to be kind of disowned by Leo at times."

"I presume you then entered the house with Richard? What happened next?" asked Eddie.

"Having called Leo from the hall and got no reply, we began looking in all the downstairs rooms at first. Finding nothing we then went upstairs and found him in the study. At first I thought he had fallen asleep on his desk but then I saw the gun in his hand. I still can't believe it. Poor Richard just stood there and sobbed his heart out," said Mel Govern, becoming emotional as he spoke. "It's so hard to believe what has happened."

"Thanks Mr Govern, we appreciate how big a blow this must be to you. We will however need you to write out a full report, just as you have told us. Come down to the station in the morning and we will have you sign it and have it recorded," said Eddie.

"Thank you Officer. If you will excuse me now, the committee have just decided to go ahead with the regatta. It's what Leo would have wanted. So many competitors have put so much effort and time into being ready for the start of the season that it would be a shame to pull the plug on it now. Leo would approve I'm sure."

Chapter 34

"That's all very strange," said Maria as they got into the car to drive back to the house. "It seems to be completely out of character. I can't see how someone, especially someone so full of life like Forrest, would leave the club in high spirits and within a short period, maybe just an hour or two, decide to kill himself. I just can't buy that. What do you think Eddie?"

"Suicide seems to be a very complex thing. God alone knows what goes on in a person's mind when they decide to end it all. I have read that once they have made the decision they become completely relaxed, believing that what they are about to do will solve not only their problems but everyone else's problems as well. I don't know if that is true or not. It certainly doesn't make a whole lot of sense to me."

"I wonder what he was really like, Eddie. You know, small town lawyer becoming a judge and leading light in the Democratic Party. Then becoming commodore of the yacht club. Do you think that if he hadn't been cleared of all involvement in the Alice Newman's case last year, that he would be still held in such high esteem?"

"Who knows, if Doctor Mackey hadn't confessed

and taken full and sole responsibility, he might have been sharing the same jail cell with Gregg Newman by now."

"Come to think of it, Gregg will soon be out. I wonder what he is going to do?" mused Eddie, "I must ask the Chief if he heard anything definite. I believe it will be hard for him to face the public here so I would anticipate him moving to another state. His political life is finished and I would think that very few would want to hire him anywhere here or in Oldtown."

By the time they got back to the house, the ambulance had just arrived to take the body to the morgue for a full autopsy. Mrs Forrest hadn't as yet arrived home due to the late arrival of her plane. When they entered the study, Simon, the pathologist was packing up his equipment and was just about to leave.

"Hi Simon, what do you think?" asked Eddie.

"Just one shot from very close range," said Simon while consulting his own notepad. "Plenty of powder burns around the wound. No exit wound so the bullet is somewhere in his brain. He was either very lucky or very unlucky, depending on the outcome he wanted. Normally a small bullet like this one could miss all the vital parts of the brain. However, in this case I would contend that he died instantly. I will have a full report tomorrow evening when I have had a chance to look inside."

"So, at what time do you estimate that he did it?"

"I would think it was probably before midnight."

"So what you are contending, if your timing is right," said Eddie, "is that Leo Forrest left the club at approximately 11.15p.m. In the best of spirits and that within 45 minutes he plugged himself! That doesn't make sense, does it?"

"I said he died, I didn't say he plugged himself." Simon's reply was frosty. "Until I complete the autopsy, everything I say is conjecture and subject to verification."

While the ambulance men were preparing to remove the body Eddie and Maria walked around the desk. It was, like everything else, a very big desk. Leo's body was slumped across it with the left side of his head resting on the desk top, the right side facing the ceiling showing the small hole in his right temple. His right hand lying, palm open across the desk with the gun in it. On the left hand side of the desk was a brandy glass lying on its side, the contents spilled on the desk. Above that was an ashtray in which a half smoked Cuban cigar lay. On the floor was a fancy looking ballpoint pen. The heavy curtain drapes were open. Leo obviously hadn't drawn them when he sat at his desk to have a nightcap and final cigar of the day.

When the ambulance men lifted the body Eddie noticed that he had fallen on a desk pad on the top of which was written Castor and Pollux. And under that were four names; Gregg Newman, Jim Mackey, Jeff Suarez and Leo Forrest and each had a line drawn through it.

"I wonder what he was thinking of?" mused Eddie, "As far as I know Castor and Pollux are two well-known stars, the ones up in the sky."

"I always thought that they were twins from Greek mythology. Something to do with Zeus!" said Maria, showing off her knowledge of ancient Greek mythology.

"You know, you might be on to something there. Leo seems to be into things connected with ancient Rome and Greece. Look at the name on this house, Vesuvius. And I noticed that the name of his yacht is Pompeii."

Making sure that the entire second floor was taped off as a crime scene and that a constant police presence would be at the house at all times, Eddie and Maria headed back to the station.

"You seem very quiet," said Maria, as they drove along the lake road. "Are you getting tired or are you getting another one of your itches? Spit it out. What are you thinking of?"

"Something is not right and I can't put my finger on it."

"So tell me. What is it?"

"The problem is that sometimes things look so

obvious that we miss what is there to be seen if we only look. So we act on assumptions. We see something, and make a judgement and then as day follows night, we follow a logical path. Ok? So far so good," said Eddie. "Now suppose our initial judgement is wrong, and then we end up going down the wrong path."

"So where do you think we may have made the wrong judgement?"

"I don't know, that's my conundrum. Everything points to suicide and so we will be concentrating on all aspects of Leo's life to see if his health was ok, if his marriage was ok, and if his finances were ok. All of these things will be examined in detail."

"But that's normal procedure, isn't it?"

"Yes, but supposing – just supposing, that Leo didn't die by suicide. Then we have a different scenario haven't we? Our process then should be different. That's what's bugging me. We didn't approach the scene from that perspective. Damn it."

"So what should we have done differently?"

"Think. We must think! Supposing someone else killed Leo. How would he or she have done it? Taking the time frame into account, they would have to be in the house when Leo got home. Wouldn't they?"

Suddenly Eddie pulled the car into a layby.

"Hold it, I need to talk to Lenny," said Eddie as he parked the car and took out his cell phone,

"Lenny, hate to spoil your Saturday afternoon but I need to ask you a question. Up to now all the indications are that Leo plugged himself, so naturally we start trying to figure out why. However, if we were to think that maybe someone else did the job, what should we be looking at? Any ideas?"

"Damn it Eddie, why do you have to complicate everything? There was no obvious evidence of a third person having been there so we are pretty sure, judging from the posture of the body and the fingerprints on the gun, that Leo did the job himself."

"But, I am just asking what if it was a third party who did it? What would you be looking for to prove my hypothesis?"

"I suppose I would be looking for imprints on the carpet and in areas where a person could have been concealed but why would we do that?" said Lenny.

"Because I think I am right. I found the piece of the jigsaw that was missing. I couldn't figure out what was wrong until now. Leo was found with the gun in his right hand, isn't that a fact?"

"Yes, but so what?"

"But Leo was left-handed."

"Christ!" exclaimed Lennie, "How did you figure that out?"

"When we were examining the house we looked at the gym he had upstairs and the golf practice unit out on the decking. Well, when I went to try my swing I found that the clubs were left-handed."

"Damn it to hell. There goes my Saturday afternoon. Maybe he was ambidextrous. Anyway, I'll get the team together and get back as soon as possible. I assume the room has been sealed off."

"Yeah, the entire first floor is sealed off. My conjecture is that it would have been possible for someone to conceal themselves behind the drapes and when Leo sat down to have his nightcap, he or she just came up behind him and killed him. If that is the case, then there must be some forensic evidence on the drapes and on the carpet behind them." he said finishing the call.

"Do you really believe that Eddie?" asked Maria.

"At this stage I'm not sure what to believe but something isn't fitting in and maybe that is what's bugging me. We do have to look at all possibilities. Maybe, as Lenny said, Leo was ambidextrous and had the brandy in his drinking hand and the gun in his right. Who knows?"

"So where do we go from here?" asked Maria.

"Well there isn't much we can do right now," said Eddie. "Lenny will update his report and we should have that first thing tomorrow. The films from the two CCTV cameras are being viewed and the gun is being checked out to see if Leo owned it. Since the house is situated on its own grounds and the nearest neighbor is half a mile away, I doubt if anyone heard gunfire last night. We have put out a request to any late revellers leaving the club after 11.00pm to come forward to be interviewed."

"What about Leo's wife, is someone going to meet her?" asked Maria.

"I understand that her son, Richard is collecting her from the airport. I have suggested to Govern that he contact Richard and have her stay with him tonight or else book her into a hotel. Staying in the home is not an option tonight. It's a crime scene."

"OK," said Maria. "I'm going to collect my boy who has turned out to be quite a competitive swimmer; he qualified for three finals today. I hope he did well. I was always afraid that with the amount of time he used to spend on his computer that he would turn out to be some kind of techy nerd."

"That's great news. What age is he now?" asked Eddie.

"He'll be eighteen next birthday. That's hard to

believe. I want him to go to college but all he wants is to become a cop, like his mother. God help him."

"Why not try and compromise?" suggested Eddie. "He goes to college for three years and then, having got his degree, he enlists as a cop. That way he has something to fall back on if the job doesn't turn out to be the bed of roses he expects."

"Yeah, I tried that but maybe he is still too young to decide on major issues like his career."

"Well, I'm off home. Shirley's Mom is with us for the weekend and we have invited a few neighbors over for a barbeque. Hope the weather stays dry. I hate trying to barbeque in the rain."

Chapter 35

The following morning, they headed across to the Chief's office for an emergency meeting. Eddie said to Maria, "Thank God he is in the temporary office. I know it isn't a very big office but I never want to be squeezed into his old box-like office ever again."

When they arrived at the office, the room seemed to be already full to capacity. The Chief, the DA Mary Donnelly with Jason Miles from her office and Lennie Bareman from forensics were all crammed around the Chief's desk. Eventually, after much pulling and shoving they managed to get two places for Eddie and Maria.

"I believe that we have a crisis. Is that fair to say?" commenced the Chief without preamble. "Our normal day-to-day workload is increasing but being handled well by all of our units. However, we seem to have a series of unsolved events that, according to Eddie, appear to be somewhat connected."

Then pulling out a number of files, he continued. "We start with the death of Angie Lummox which is still unsolved. This was followed on the same day by the death of Doctor Mitchum, which appears to have been an unfortunate accident. Then, more recently, we have had the death of Jeff Suarez, another accident. And now we have the apparent suicide of Leo Forrest. Now to my way of thinking, that is too many coincidences and I believe that when there are too many coincidences, they are no longer coincidences. So, as of now, all leave is suspended until such time as we find out what the hell is going on! Eddie, can you bring us up to date on progress."

"Yes Chief. As you know, we found a sheet of paper under Forrest's body when it was being removed. On it was written a list of four people with a line drawn through each one," said Eddie while handing a copy of the list around the table. "Now reverting to the list of incidents mentioned by the Chief, I do believe that there is some sort of tenuous link between three of the incidents. I am not too sure about the fourth incident, the death of Doctor Mitchum."

"However, if we look at the other three... Leo Forrest is connected to Jeff Suarez, both being members of the Democratic Party and also members of the Election for Mayor Committee. In addition, Jeff Suarez, Leo Forrest and Doctor Mackey were part of what was called The Wolf Pack on a recent TV show. Doctor Mackey and Gregg Newman are both in prison. That leaves Al McNally and Teddy Moran the Chairman of the Oldtown Farmers Bank, and Mark Reilly Gregg Newman's boss, untouched." Then consulting his notes, he said, "Now if we look at Gregg

RETRIBUTION FOR ALICE

Newman, in whose house Angie Lummox was murdered, he is connected to both Forrest and Suarez, having been the Democratic candidate for the election until they dumped him. The question in his case is – was he set up and if so by whom? Finally, Doctor Mitchum was Gregg Newman's wife Alice's psychiatrist. So where does he fit in?"

"That's a lot of questions," interjected the DA, "but have you any answers?"

At this stage the atmosphere in the office was becoming unbearable – hot and stuffy.

"Damn this office!" said the Chief, with beads of perspiration on his ever-reddening face. "We hardly have space to take notes let alone do a brainstorm on a white board. Where would we put it even if we had one?"

"Can I suggest," said Eddie "that we get some fresh air and reconvene this meeting in fifteen minutes' time in my office? There we will have space to breath and we do have white boards and anything else we may need."

"Now that makes sense. Another ten minutes in this office and we will all be inhaling pure carbon dioxide." said the Chief.

Twenty minutes later, having taken a coffee break, they were all comfortably seated in the conference room beside Eddie's office.

When the meeting reconvened the Chief started by saying, "Before we left my office Mary, you had asked Eddie a question. You wanted to know if we had any answers to those questions that he had put to us. Well, Eddie has a theory so let's see what you make of it. Ok Eddie, tell them what you think."

"My theory is that Gregg Newman was set up by someone unknown. I believe that it was neither his own party nor the opposition party that were involved, based on the outcome of the election. We also know that he has been found not guilty by the court. So who did it and why? Furthermore, we now know that his wife couldn't have done it as we have proof that she was elsewhere at the time of the murder."

Taking a marker, Eddie wrote on the whiteboard: Who killed Angie Lummox and who could benefit from Gregg being found guilty of her death?

Then, still standing at the board, like a lecturer, he said, "OK let's leave that for the moment and move on and look at Doctor Mitchum's accident. I believe that Doctor Mitchum's death was murder. But I don't think that was the intended target; rather it was Alice Newman who was the target. Why do I say that? Well, we now know that someone knew exactly what Alice was doing every time she borrowed the doctor's car. So, if we believe her and I do, we know that on that fateful day a note was put in the car instructing her where to go and where to park the car – in the basement level of the mall car park. I believe that either the car's brakes or power steering were interfered with there."

"Unfortunately, it was when the doctor was, for some unknown reason, rushing home that something went wrong with the car and it crashed over the barriers. Doctor Mitchum was a normally a very careful man in all he did. It would have been completely out of character for him to create such an accident. Therefore, it had to be Alice who was the intended victim." Once again he wrote on the board: Who had the opportunity and who would benefit from Alice's death?

"Next we come to Jeff Suarez's death. Accident? Maybe but my gut tells me no. Suarez walked around that scaffolding at least three, if not four nights every week. When he finished his tour, he was usually seen to be resting his arms on the traverse bar and looking out over the city. He was a stickler for security and always made sure that he had his hard hat on when visiting the site. It is unlikely that the scaffold traverse bar was not secured or became loose in all the months that it was there."

So, writing for the third time, he wrote: Who would benefit from Suarez' death?

"Finally I believe that Leo Forrest was also murdered; a left-handed person doesn't use his right hand to kill himself. So the fourth question is: Who benefits from his death and why go to the trouble of making it look like suicide?"

"Also, if I am right, Teddy Moran, Mark Reilly and Al McNally's lives might be at risk."

"Thanks Eddie. I sincerely hope you are wrong." said the Chief.

"I think it would be no harm to set up a meeting with Moran, McNally and Reilly, just to warn them and get their views on what could be happening." said Eddie.

"If Eddie is right, we could be looking at a conspiracy against a specific group," said the DA. "But we don't have any real evidence to support that. What I see is purely conjecture. It sounds plausible, but unless we can come up with some breakthrough to substantiate your hypotheses, we are back to square one."

"Lennie, your squad has examined all four sites. What do you think?" asked the Chief.

"Well, whoever killed Angie left absolutely no trail that we could find. He or she was very clear on what they intended and very clever in carrying it out. Namely, to kill a young girl in cold-blood with the intention of having Gregg Newman found guilty of the crime. For which he would spend a long period of his life in prison - the death penalty having been abolished in this state five years ago."

"Yes, very cold and calculating." said the DA

"But," continued Lennie, "why go to all that trouble? Why not just have him shot?"

"A very good point," interjected Eddie, "that would seem to indicate that the objective was not just to even a score with Gregg. It could be an attempt to discredit him or people he associated with, such as the Party."

"But why then try and kill Alice?" asked the Chief. "No one knew where she was at that time. And apart from her psychiatrist, she wasn't talking to anyone."

"I have always felt that Alice was central to all that was going on." said Maria. "I think it would be very worthwhile having another conversation with her. It's possible that without knowing it, she has some information that would help us, and was seen as a threat to others?"

"Good thinking," said the Chief who turned to Eddie and asked him to mark in opposite his first item on the board: Interview Alice again. "That covers item one and two, for the time being."

"It might be no harm to have a chat with Joe Breslin, Gregg's defence attorney." said the DA. "He gave a very robust defence at Gregg's trial and appeared to have uncovered a number of possible sightings of suspicious activity in the area around Gregg's house at the time. I think it is time for us to actively follow these leads up."

"Good idea Mary, mark that up on the board Eddie," said the Chief. "What's next?"

"Next on the list we have Doctor Mitchum," said Eddie. "In this case we have a partial image from one of the CCTV cameras in the clinic which would appear to show a female approaching his car before Alice got into it. Unfortunately, we haven't been able to identify that person. We do however have a slight suspicion that the ex-assistant matron, Jane Starling, might be involved in some way. We have interviewed her but I think we need to put some pressure on her. In the meantime, she has transferred to the Haven Clinic up in Wayward Creek and we are checking her out up there. She seems to have adopted a new persona and a transformation in appearance since she went there."

"Ok, who is following that up?" asked the Chief.

"We are currently using three of the additional squad you allocated to our unit. They are checking out every possible connection she is making and also her banking and phone records." replied Eddie.

"Good. Next we have Jeff Suarez's accident," said the Chief. "What's the position with this?"

"Up to now all the indications were that his fall was purely an accident. Forensics examined the scaffolding and found that one of the traverse bars had been fitted incorrectly and had come loose when Suarez leaned on it. As a result, it just gave way when he leaned on it and he fell off the platform," said Lennie, "an apparent accident. However, I know from experience that these bars are designed so that the end of the traverse bar fits around the upright, like a cupped hand, making it almost impossible for the bar to fall outwards, even if the retaining screws were loose. And," continued Lennie, "Since we have heard that he was often seen leaning on that bar, having a smoke, on many previous occasions whoever fitted it must have been very careless. Or someone deliberately interfered with it. The insurance company's findings were that it was an accident due to the incorrect fitting of one of the traverse bars of the scaffolding. We now know that the scaffolding firm and their insurers intend to vigorously fight that finding."

"Finally," began Eddie, "we come to Leo Forrest. Once again someone had very good inside information. Someone who knew that he would be home alone. Someone who knew the CCTV coverage or lack of it. But the big question I have is why make it look like a suicide and what, if anything did the writing on his desk pad mean? Castor and Pollux with the list of names?"

"Personally I think we are grasping at straws." said the DA. "For instance, if we look at the supposition that the scaffolding was interfered with, how could that have been possible with the desk sergeant watching the site on CCTV?"

"If I wanted to do it I would get someone to call to the station and distract the sergeant with some spurious complaint. Do you think that would be possible?" countered Eddie. "Remember how short staffed we are. It could easily be done."

"Look Eddie, a lot of what you have said makes sense, but without a breakthrough it is only speculation. Prove one supposition and the rest might fall into place." replied the Chief.

"We are due a break," said Eddie, "I feel it is on its way."

"OK let's get cracking. I want these cases solved and solved fast," said the Chief as he called the meeting to an end.

Chapter 36

The following morning when Eddie got to his office he found a note to say that Tim Bradshaw was looking for him and asking him to call back.

"Now isn't that a bit of a coincidence," muttered Eddie, as he picked up the phone to call him. "Number one on our list and Tim comes to us!"

"Maybe this is the breakthrough we were waiting for." said Maria, who had just entered his office.

"Good morning Mr Bradshaw. I believe you were looking for me," said Eddie as soon as Bradshaw had answered the call.

"Yes indeed, you asked me to call you if Alice remembered anything that might be of help in your investigations. Well, it may not be anything of substance but she is getting some flashbacks, recalls and I think it might be worth your while listening to her."

"Certainly we would love to. When and where can we meet her?"

"She has an appointment with me for tomorrow morning at ten a.m. we could schedule you in for, say, eleven thirty a.m. Would that suit you?"

"That's perfect. See you at your office and thanks. I

appreciate you getting back to us."

Then turning to Maria he said,

"I don't know what she wants to tell us but I do know what I want to ask her. What does she know that makes her a danger to somebody? Let's hope she remembers what it is."

"So much of what happened to her in her life with Gregg must have been in a haze of drink or depression. It must have been a very traumatic time for her," replied Maria.

The following morning exactly at eleven thirty, Eddie and Maria were entering the offices of Menzies and Steen which were located on Tavern Street in the old part of the town. The building had a brightly painted clapboard frontage, in keeping with the other buildings on the street, most of which were business offices. When they first set up their business Makenzie & Steen had rented one room on the third floor of the building. Now they owned the entire building and occupied all three floors. It was Eddie's first time to visit the building and he was very impressed by what he saw. There was nothing ostentatious about the place. The first impression they got when they entered the foyer was of quiet efficiency. The waiting room they were brought into was pleasantly comfortable with a six-foot-long aquarium on one wall with what appeared to be a multitude of colored fish going about their fishy business. In the background classical music played quietly.

"Good morning Detectives and thank you for coming," said Bradshaw as he shook hands with both of them. "I see our fish have interested you. The psychology guys tell us that just watching them swimming around the tank relaxes our clients. Some people, they say, get very uptight having to visit an attorney or a dentist. Would you believe that?"

Then leading the way, he brought them to a long conference room in which Alice Newman was already seated. Once the handshakes had taken place and all were seated around the table, Bradshaw said. "As I mentioned to you on the phone yesterday, Ms Newman has been making great progress in her rehabilitation; so much so that she is beginning to have vivid flashbacks of some events that happened prior to her hospitalization. Now some of her recall may be somewhat vague and others may be irrelevant to your enquiries. I have taken notes on the issues that I feel you would want to know about. However rather than read them out to you I feel it is important that Alice actually tells you herself. So let's listen to what she has to say and hopefully she will still have recall. Sometimes she remembers something only to forget it again. Then maybe she will take questions. Is that okay?"

With Bradshaw prompting her, a lot of what she had to say was in relation to her marriage and Gregg's changing attitudes to her especially around the time he was nominated to run for City Mayor. She also talked at length about her love for her daughter Tracey who she said had kept her in the marriage when all else appeared to have gone. She then went on to talk about her relationship with Doctor Mitchum whom she said had saved her life and her sanity. He firmly believed in her and was determined to have her released. She also recalled instances when both the Matron and her assistant had gone beyond normal practices in order to support her. Then when it appeared that she had talked herself out, Eddie said, "You mentioned that at times when The Wolf Pack would visit your house you would not be privy to any of their discussions. However, you did mention that on occasions you did eavesdrop on them. Can you remember anything that you may have heard that struck you as odd?"

"No, not really." she replied. "You see they used our house as a kind of secure place to plot and scheme and have a few drinks without having to worry about who would see them together. On other nights they would play poker until early morning. On those nights Gregg would join them but I would have nothing to do with them. They looked after their own drinks. However, on other nights when I would be serving them drinks they would usually, but not always, clam up as soon as I entered the room. On some such occasions I would know, by just looking at them, that they were having an argument. Now that I think of it, it was on one such occasion that, as soon as I left the room and closed the door behind me, I snuck back and listened. That was one of the times that Gregg caught me and hit me hard and warned me that if the others knew I had listened that what they would do to me would be a lot more than what he did."

"Sorry to push this," said Maria, "but have you any recall as to what they were arguing about?"

"Let me think... No, I'm afraid it is blocked out. It's hanging around the back of my head but it won't move forward, if that makes any sense."

"Don't worry, it will come to you later," said Bradshaw.

"Thanks. Sometimes I get a full recall and then before I know it, it just disappears again. It's hard to explain. Just now I can see them all as I was leaving the room, their faces flushed, all standing – no – all except for the one they were facing. Then when I had just left the room I heard them shouting. I had sneaked back to the door to listen. But what were they shouting? Damn it! What, what?"

"Take it easy Alice," said Bradshaw, "maybe, if you wrote down their names and then visualize them in your mind, some more detail might come to you."

"Well, of course there was Leo with his stinking cigars. He was the only one who ever had the cheek to smoke in our house. No such thing as please or may I? He just puffed and puffed. It always took days to get the smell out of the house, even by using scented candles. What an arrogant man!"

"Very good, now who else was there?"

"There was chubby Teddy, the banker and beside him was big tall Al with the old fashioned fountain pen in his top pocket. I bet it was never used, just there for show. Maybe that was a trait of all attorneys? Of course Jeff with his sleek black hair and his Mexican looks. I can see him with both of his hands gripping the back of a chair. He looked really angry, and yes the good Doctor Jim; he had his hand on Jeff's shoulder as if to contain him. And Gregg's boss, the silent Mark with the shifty eyes. Oh yes, the other guy just sat in the chair looking very worried. He wasn't a regular and had just joined them to do something about a report. That's it, exclaimed Alice. They were shouting about a report that wasn't finished, or something like that, and I heard them say something about a son ending up in serious trouble if it wasn't completed.

Does any of that make sense? Maybe the son was to have completed whatever they were waiting for?"

"Yes, Alice, every little piece of information is important, it's like a jigsaw," said Eddie, "and it is surprising how one small piece brings the big picture together. Certainly your information makes a lot of sense to us. If you can remember the person's name it would be of immense help to us. In the meantime, I'm sure Gregg will be able to help us in this regard."

Then, seeing that Alice was getting stressed, Eddie thanked her for all her help and wished her a swift and complete recovery.

"If Alice recalls anything else of interest I will call you again," said Bradshaw as he ushered them to the door.

"I wonder if 'chubby' Moran will be as helpful when we visit him?" said Eddie, as they headed for their car which was in a car park, two streets away. The narrow streets in the old part of the town were never built to cater for street parking. "He is number two on our list of people to interview."

Chapter 37

Getting an appointment with Teddy Moran wasn't an easy thing to arrange, or maybe giving an interview to the police wasn't on his bucket list. Whatever the reason was, Teddy Moran was not available to meet them until the following Thursday when he could spare thirty minutes only. In addition, he said that it would expedite matters greatly if they could tell him what exactly they were looking for. To which Eddie had answered 'Security, your security.'

"OK, while we are waiting for Moran that leaves Starling, Breslin, McNally and Reilly to be interviewed. Let's see who is available." said Eddie.

Ten minutes later Eddie and Maria were on their way to the Minerva Clinic. Matron Sue Smyth was available for the next hour only. She was then heading south for a late Fall vacation.

"If we keep visiting you at this rate, people will begin to think that we are receiving treatment," said Eddie as Matron Smyth greeted them at the clinic.

"You are always welcome. The police have always been very generous in supporting our fundraising activities. Now how can we help you today Detective?" Matron smiled.

"In actual fact, what we are looking for is information on Jane Starling."

"Jane Starling? Oh my! Has she been up to mischief?"

"Nothing that we know of, Matron, but we realize that we know very little about her and hope that you can fill us in on her background: where did she come from? Does she have family and anything else that you may know about." said Maria.

"Hold on there, and I will pull her personnel file and see what we have on her, and see how much I can share with you," said matron as she left the office to fetch the file.

A little later all three of them were hunched around the desk examining Starling's file. They now knew that she was forty-two years old and had been married prior to being employed by the clinic. Something nobody seemed to be aware of. She had no children. She had been born in Florida and had a business qualification. According to a note in her file she had two brothers. When her father died the three children went to live with their mother and when she died they moved on. Her hobbies were all sporting and outdoor activities and, surprisingly, she held a black belt in martial arts. Other than that the file told them nothing else.

"Did she ever confide in you about her family?" asked Maria.

"Come to think of it, she never did talk about them,"

matron said, "I know that on some of her weekends off, she used to go to Watsonville. I got the impression, or maybe she mentioned something about it, that she was visiting one of her brothers who lived there. In all the time she was here she was a very efficient assistant but a kind of reserved person. She was just there, if you know what I mean. She didn't stand out in any way and never took part in any of our social activities. She was just a plain Jane, I suppose."

"Did she ever have boyfriends or girlfriends?" asked Maria.

"No, not that I was aware of."

Having thanked matron, they headed back to the station.

"Well that was interesting," began Eddie, "Plain Jane had no personality and no romantic association for all of her time at the Minerva. Then voilá, she moves to the Haven, adopts a different persona, and within a few months has a boyfriend. Does that make sense to you?"

"Strange things do happen but no, something does not sound right to me. The other thing that interested me was the bit about the brother. I think a call to the station in Watsonville is called for. The name Starling isn't a very common one so it shouldn't be hard to find out about him." said Maria.

"That's strange," said Eddie, fifteen minutes later as he hung up the phone. "According to patrolman McCuskey in Watsonville, he couldn't find anyone of that name living in the town and he said he has lived there all of his life. Matron must have got it wrong."

"What's strange?" asked Lennie as he walked in to the office and perched his backside on the edge of Eddie's desk. "If you ask me, I think everything about this case is strange."

"Maybe we shouldn't ask you." said Eddie with a smile on his face. Before Lennie could reply he continued, "Ok, before the weekend is upon us, and the Chief kicks ass, let's try and firm up on our interviews with Joe Breslin, Al McNally and Mark Reilly and get them all finished. Just remember we have Teddy Moran slotted in for Thursday next. Maria, you try Joe and I'll try Al."

Eddie had just put on his jacket and was about to head home when his cell phone rang.

"Hi Detective, Bradshaw here. Just wanted to let you know that Alice recalled the other guy's name. It was Joey something or other. She recalls one of the others shouting 'you have to do it Joey.' I hope that means something and will help you."

"Well at least we now know that his name is Joey. But Joey who?"

By the time they finished for the day they had managed to finalize all of the interviews for that week. They had arranged the interviews with Breslin and McNally for the Wednesday and Joe Breslin was to call to the station at nine thirty a.m. on the Friday. Al McNally had agreed to meet them at his office at twelve noon on the same day. Mark Reilly was out of town and due back on the Friday. His secretary would confirm his availability when he made contact with his office the following day. Things were beginning to move.

Chapter 38

At exactly nine forty a.m. Joe Breslin rushed into Eddie's office looking hot and flustered. "My apologies for being late. I forgot that your unit had relocated away from the old building. What a mess out there, it is like a scrap car depot, cars parked at random. Any idea when the building will be completed?"

"No, every time we ask we get a different answer," replied Eddie. "There always seems to be a reason for another delay. Well if they don't finish soon our Chief will have a stroke and that's for sure."

"By the way, Eddie I watched your junior team beat ours on Saturday." said Breslin. "Nice win. I must admit that you have done a great job coaching them. Pity about your knee, if you hadn't damaged it I am sure you could have gone all the way yourself."

"No going back now. The damage is irreparable. Anyway at my age the young ones would run rings around me!" laughed Eddie.

"Now you mentioned in your call that you were interested in our evidence relating to sightings in and around Newman's house around the time of the incident." said Joe.

"Yeah, we think that you might have information that you gleaned when you were defending Gregg Newman on that murder charge…."

"A charge that we emphatically refuted – and won!" interjected Joe.

"I know. I know that, relax. We are not in any way questioning the outcome of that case. However, we still need to find out who did it. So, in your defence you produced evidence of sightings of various people and vehicles. Evidence, I must confess, that we didn't find. However, we would now like to follow up on anything that you can provide us with. Even things that you didn't use during the case."

"Certainly, I can see no conflict of interest in doing that. However, Eddie, if I do hand over my file, you will owe me one. Deal?"

"Yeah, ok. You got yourself a deal."

With that, Joe opened his briefcase and produced a wad of sworn testimonies. "Have a quick look through these and I want them back intact. No photocopying!"

"Thanks Joe, I really appreciate this."

"By the way I hear rumors that wedding bells will be ringing soon, any truth?"

"Yeah, the plan is set for August next and Shirley and her mother are in their element working out all of the details. Her mother is so excited and, as she says, she is now looking forward to having grandchildren. She must know something that I don't! Now and again I am roped in to give my blessing on some detail or other. Shirley is, like me, not too impressed by wedding planners and all of that kind of stuff. To our way of thinking, once the formal ceremony is over, it is just a great opportunity to celebrate with our friends and that celebration doesn't have to be in a posh hotel. In actual fact we are having it in Mario's and hopefully nobody will fall off the decking into the lake!"

When Joe had left the office after suggesting to Eddie that they get together for a drink some evening, Eddie handed the file to Maria.

"Maria, pass these on to Dan Crosier, will you? I'm sure his squad will appreciate the break from checking up on Starling's phone records and the mall car park scanned records. Oh and tell them it is urgent. Ask them to drop everything and analyse these testimonies under two headings – sightings of persons and sighting of vehicles."

"For your sake, Eddie, I hope that when Joe calls in his deal – which I have no doubt that he will – it won't compromise you!" laughed Maria as she headed out to the squad room.

By the time she returned Eddie realized that they were running tight for their interview with McNally.

"Get your jacket on, we better be on our way to McNally's office. Traffic can be very slow at this time of day." said Eddie to Maria.

How right he was, a journey that would normally take thirty minutes took almost forty-five leaving them with five minutes to spare. Luckily there was a parking spot just across the street from the office.

"Sometimes you are lucky, sometimes you are not!" said Eddie as they exited the car and ran to the office.

On their way to the meeting they had agreed on their tactics. Eddie would emphasize the possible danger that McNally was in and Maria would hone in on The Wolf Pack and try and find out who Joey was.

Even though McNally's office was in the old part of the city, his office was luxurious in comparison to the police station. The walls were finished in rich walnut paneling to match the enormous desk that McNally sat behind, which he didn't leave to greet his visitors. His demeanor was that of a cat watching a mouse.

"So, to what do I owe the honor of this visit Detective?" was his opening greeting, while making an obvious glance at his watch. "I have a very busy schedule so, what's this all about?"

"In the first instance, we want to thank you for taking

the time to see us Mr McNally. We also have a very busy day trying to solve crimes and trying to prevent them from occurring. So we will be as brief as possible," said Maria, switching the attention away from Eddie. McNally had deliberately tried to exclude Maria from his gaze. This was to be a man to man show.

"Yes I appreciate that," said McNally, again addressing Eddie.

"I'm sure you are aware of the tragic series of events that have occurred in the past few weeks," said Maria, establishing her equal part in the interview. "First we had Suarez's accident and then Forrest's suicide. Now we don't want to alarm you, but when we put all the pieces together, starting with Gregg Newman, we find a common thread running through it all – the Democratic Mayoral Election Committee. If you include Gregg in the pot you will find that two are in prison and two are dead. That leaves only Moran, Reilly and yourself and we feel it is our duty to warn you that your life may be in danger and to advise you to take certain precautions." said Maria.

"Are you serious? An accident and a suicide, and you jump to these conclusions? What kind of deductive reasoning is that?" McNally appeared incredulous.

"Maybe you are right but we have warned you and we will also be warning Moran and Reilly. Is there anyone else of your group that might need to be warned?"

"No, absolutely not."

"What about the other member of your group, Joey?" asked Maria.

What Eddie observed was a man taking a knockout punch. For a moment the color left his face before he regained his composure. "Joey? Who is he?" he blustered, bringing the blood rushing back to his face.

"You don't know of him?" said Eddie. "That's surprising. We know that you met him on a number of occasions in Gregg Newman's house. Maybe that will jog your memory."

"As I said, I don't know who you are talking about. Now, if you will excuse me, I have a meeting to attend. Good day to you."

As they made their way back down to the lobby they both agreed that they had probably succeeded in ruining McNally's day for him; he was now a very worried man. Whether that was due to the possible threat on his life or because they had hit a nerve. Both agreed that it was the nerve. But why? He wasn't the kind of person to be easily unnerved.

"Let's try the same on 'chubby' Teddy tomorrow. I bet you he will be prepared. No doubt McNally will have contacted him to warn him." said Eddie.

While McNally's office oozed of opulence and grandeur, Teddy Moran's office was the opposite. A functional desk and three chairs facing it and one filing cabinet in the corner. One large photo of a number of men in suits adorned the wall behind him. Too far away for both Eddie and Maria to identify who they were. That was it! He would always say that when people invested their money in his bank they appreciated the obvious fact that the bank didn't spend their money on unproductive trimmings. Also the fact that he (Moran) hadn't followed the makers and shakers up to Oakville went down well with his customers. In his own eyes he remained a country boy at heart, faithful to his roots and his people. When asked how he came to make his fortune, he would answer 'Investment son, shrewd investment. Invest your money with the Farmers Bank and you can't go wrong.' But however he did it, he had risen from the position of lowly bank clerk, living in a rented one room apartment on the outskirts of the town, to becoming manager at the early age of thirty-six before becoming CEO six years later with a six-bedroomed, purpose-built mansion on a fifty-acre estate one mile outside the town.

As soon as Eddie and Maria were seated, Moran rang his secretary to bring in some coffee for Eddie and Maria.

"You know Detectives, I am still in shock at the death of two of my oldest friends." Moran began. "Do you know that we all grew up together here in Oldtown and we had such good times then? We even went to college in Wayward Creek at the same time." Standing up to point to the photo on the wall he continued, "that photo was taken in our final year and now two of us are gone. What's happening?"

"Yes, it's hard to believe what is happening but in actual fact, that is the purpose of our visit. We want to formally advise you to take precautions from now on. Too many of your close friends are having what could be called a run of bad luck." said Eddie.

"Do you really think I am in danger?" Moran's eyebrows rose in disbelief.

"We don't know what to think but it is always safer to err on the safe side, don't you agree," said Maria. Now out of the group that used to meet in Newman's house, Suarez and Forrest are dead and Newman and Mackey are in prison. That leaves you, McNally, Reilly and possibly Joey in danger. If I were you I would want all the protection I could get until we solve a few things."

"You really are serious, aren't you Detective?" Moran's concern was evident.

"Yes we are," Maria replied, "and we are also advising every one of your group to take precautions. Unfortunately, we don't have contact details for Joey, do you?"

"Joey? I can't recall anyone of that name." Moran

frowned and shook his head. "You see over the years we had occasion to invite individuals to advise us of investments and perhaps he fitted into that category." He said absent-mindedly scratching his head. "Have you any idea when he was with us? I really have no recall of a Joey being with us detective. Someone must have been mistaken. By the way, where did you get that idea? Oh maybe I shouldn't ask that kind of question. In the meantime, if I recall anything further I will contact you immediately."

On the drive back to Oakville as they tried to pull all the strings from the two interviews together without success, Eddie complained about the lack of resources they had. "What a difference it would have made if only we could have put a tap on this guy's phones." mused Eddie.

"There is no way we could get that without due cause." replied Maria. They needed a break. It was obvious that both Moran and McNally had something to hide and that something might be the key to discovering who killed Forrest and possibly Suarez. Once again it all came back to Alice. Did she really know more than she thought she did? On the other hand, if they asked Gregg he would certainly know, but could they ask him and would he help if it might implicate him in whatever was going on? The DA would be the person to advise them. Then, the questions surrounding Starling needed to be answered. It was time to find out who she really was and what her background was.

In the meantime, Eddie was getting more frustrated with the lack of progress. "I know this is all tied together. I just can't see it yet." muttered Eddie.

When they got back to the office there was a note to contact Dan Crosier.

"What's up Dan?" asked Eddie, as he walked into the room that had been set aside for the extra squad assigned to help out with the investigations. Their job was to plough through all of the data that was being assembled from the CCTV cameras and the mall cark park, not to mention the phone and bank records.

"I think we have found something interesting. Look at this. We have been looking through the records of the scanning machine in the mall car park for the specific time you requested and listing anything that stood out as different. We weren't sure exactly what to expect and I suppose we weren't disappointed at finding nothing until we noticed one car that entered and exited twice during that time. Now that in itself might mean nothing. However, when we dropped that exercise, as you requested, and began to analyse the testimonies that Joe Breslin gave us. And what do you know, four of the witnesses had mentioned seeing a Ford Taurus acting suspiciously around Gregg's house. Unfortunately, none of them were able to give a full registration number of the car. All could give only partial numbers. However, when we look at each of the partial numbers they all fitted in with the number of the car at the mall. Was that a coincidence? I don't think so." said Dan. "We are now tracing the registered owner and should have that within the hour."

"Well done, Dan, and please pass on our congratulations to the squad member who spotted it. Good detective work."

It was actually two hours later that Dan came back to Eddie's office, "The registered owner is a Sean Stenson with an address here in Oakville. I have one of our colleagues checking his address."

"Great! Let me know when he gets back to you and, again, well done." said Eddie.

Chapter 39

"Hi honey, we just have to celebrate," said Shirley, flinging her arms around Eddie's neck as he arrived home that evening. "You will never guess what news I just got—actually two pieces of news. Go on guess.... No! Let me tell you. We just got word from the Governor's office that the law is going to be changed and all inmates of psychiatric facilities, whether currently in the system or committed in the future, will have the right to have their committal reviewed every three years, enshrined in legislation. We have won! We have won much more than we expected. No one believed that any change in the law would apply retrospectively to those already in the system. It just shows you, Eddie, what can be achieved when the media work together!" beamed Shirley.

"Well done Shirley! I know that the Chronicle and NTTV were the big hitters in this but without your energy and belief it would never have happened. I am so proud of you!"

"Thanks Eddie. I'm sure Doctor Mitchum, if he had lived to see what he started coming to fruition, would have been thrilled. Alice will appreciate it for him."

"So now all you have to do is to try and identify

those who are in the system and see that their voices are heard." Eddie paused, "and what is the second piece of good news?"

"You won't believe it Eddie! Butch has decided to run the Chat with Shirley show weekly, starting next week! Would you believe it?"

"That's fantastic and well done! It's a pity we have no champagne in the fridge but we do have beer." said Eddie, as he pulled two beers from the fridge.

On the following Tuesday night's Chat with Shirley program, Shirley announced the good news regarding their campaign. She then followed up with a sparkling interview with Don Harding and Butch Collins whom she praised for their courage in initiating and spearheading the campaign.

"It is the very core value of NTTV to flush out the truth whenever we can and not to be afraid of adverse comments." said Butch. Putting his arm on Don's broad shoulder he said, "And this is a value that we here in NTTV learned at a very early time in our existence from our good friends in the Oldtown Chronicle."

When closing the show Shirley proudly announced that the show was now to be a weekly show and that the next show would be on the social effects of towns expanding to become cities. As Shirley was walking out of the studio and was in conversation with both Butch and Don, she was now being treated as an equal despite her young age, her cell phone rang.

"You still haven't done anything about the elephant in the room, have you?" said the quiet voice, the voice that still haunted her from the first time she heard it.

"Don't hang up please. I really want to find the elephant but so far nobody seems to know anything about it. What should I know?"

"You're the reporter, check out who initiated the report on the unsuitability of the original freeway route and follow it all the way from Oldtown to the Governor's office. Do you really believe it was a chance report? People were hurt, good people were destroyed. Good luck. I know you can do it. I have faith in you."

"Please don't hang up. Oh damn it, he's gone." muttered Shirley re-joining her two interviewees.

"What was that all about?" asked Butch.

Having relayed to them the content of the phone call she then filled them in on her efforts to find out more about the report and who the author was. However, all that she had succeeded in finding out was that the man who wrote the report was a Joseph Herbert Ashton from Watsonville and that he had died by suicide. Later on she had discovered that he had left a wife, who had passed away only last year, and three children, but beyond that she got nowhere. Having listened to Shirley, both Butch and Don agreed that in keeping with what both had just said on the program, this was something that needed to be investigated fully, no matter what the consequences.

But where to start? As Shirley had pointed out, the man who had written the report was dead, as was his wife. That left only his children but even if they were located, what would they possibly know of their fathers' work?

At the time that the freeway rerouting was taking place the NTTV station did not exist. However at the time both Butch and Don were reporters with the Oldtown Chronicle. Both would have been reporting on developments in the area. The problem was did any of the records of their findings still exist?

"Say Don, why don't you go and check up on your archives and see what you can dig up," said Butch. "I will send one of our reporters to Watsonville to see what we can find out about Joseph Herbert Ashton and his family. At least that is a starting point."

"Sure, no problem, but don't hold your breath. Oldtown hasn't a good reputation for record keeping!"

Two days later the three of them got together to report on progress.

Much to Don's disappointment, he had nothing positive to report. He couldn't find anything in the Chronicle archives. He then examined the records in the local library and could only find coverage of reaction to the changes that were envisaged and a short biography of Joseph Ashton. Nothing that they didn't know already. There was nothing unusual or controversial in any of the coverage.

Butch was much more successful. It was at the local police station that his reporter had hit gold. The older white-haired station sergeant remembered Mr Ashton very well. He was a very gentle man if ever there was one, he recalled, famous and much sought after all over the state. He would be employed by most of the big construction companies before they would buy land on which to build. He said that what had happened was a terrible double tragedy; "I don't know how his wife Meg survived it all," he said. Apparently his youngest son, Karl, the one with the brightest future ahead of him, was arrested on a charge of aggravated assault during his father's funeral. He had accosted a businessman who had attended the funeral and blamed him for his father's death, physically attacking him. The sergeant didn't believe that the young man had inflicted much damage to the man. None the less, he was convicted and sentenced to one month in prison. His other brother Max had joined the army which the sergeant reckoned was inevitable bearing in mind the fact that the army base was just outside of town and all the young fellas would be in awe of the soldiers strutting around the town. The only surprise was that both hadn't enlisted. He heard at some stage that he had been sent over to Iraq and never came back to Watsonville. If you want to find him try the army, he had suggested. They must have an address for him if he is still alive and drawing his army pension. Finally, he said that the daughter, Mary Jane had married a soldier who, like her brother, was sent to Iraq during the Desert Storm campaign, but couldn't say if he ever came back or not.

"So who was the guy the young lad hit?" asked Don.

"There must be a court record of the case," replied Butch, "but is that really worth following up? I would suggest that we concentrate on finding out where they all are now. They might be able to give us some information that could help us. In the meantime, let's see if we can find out who commissioned the survey and more importantly, find out who signed off on the rerouting."

"Yes," said Shirley, "that is the key to unlocking the problem. Someone in the Governor's office knows the full story. Now who has the sort of influence with that administration that can help us?"

"I suppose we could approach our Mayor, Erin Sullivan and see if she would be willing to help. On the other hand, we could approach someone in the Republican Party, they might be more interested in scoring points." said Don.

"Why not try both and see what happens?" said Shirley.

"You know something," said Butch while absently rubbing his chin with his hand, "this is beginning to stink. But I also smell a good story. I think it is time to take it very carefully. First things first. Let's get our legal boys in on it and see if we can really get to the bottom of it – or should I say the top of it - if it really goes to the Governor's office."

"Who was the Governor at the time?" asked Shirley.

"I think it was Jed Wilks," replied Don, "and a right shifty guy he was, in my opinion. He lasted only one period in office before Mel Nolan, polling on a 'Clean up the Governor's office' campaign, had him drummed out of office."

Finally, the legal departments in both the Chronicle and NTTV having got together gave their opinion. It was their view that it would be not be in the commercial interests of NTTV and the Chronical to commence, or indeed to continue with any sort of investigation into the events that resulted in the rerouting of the freeway. The opined that there was a very definite risk, having regard of the public standing of those who were possibly involved of them initiating legal proceedings; proceedings that could take many years to bring to a conclusion. However, having said that, they went on to say that, from the information that had been gleaned, particularly having regard to the suicide of the report writer, it would be well within their rights to suggest that the overall events that led to the decision being taken, should be examined by way of an independent judicial enquiry. They had gone on to say that the television program that NTTV had recently broadcast regarding Oldtown would be an ideal foundation to use to commence the campaign to have such an enquiry. As a matter of fact, it would be possible to use the extensive feedback they had received to authenticate their proposal as being in the public interest.

Finally, they cautioned that the program would have to be vetted in advance to ensure that all they were doing was reflecting the views of the public. This would have to be thought out very carefully and they had no doubt that it should be orchestrated using the ever more popular Chat with Shirley program. Once again the Chronical and NTTV were about to rock the boat all the way to the Governor's office. They were becoming the voice of the people in the state. As a result, their advertising revenue was beginning to noticeably increase as did their circulation figures.

When Shirley was advised of the decision she was delighted. Her anonymous phone caller would now see that she was seriously looking for the elephant in the room. Immediately they set about putting together a plan to play off articles and comments strategically placed in the Chronicle. Once that was in place NTTV would introduce a phone-in slot with well-prepared questions being submitted by concerned citizens. If that didn't raise awareness, nothing would. In which case they would have to develop a second plan. However, their reporting instincts told them that they were on the right track and they weren't wrong.

By the end of the second program, with Shirley expertly choreographing the exchanges, the station's switchboard was inundated with callers commenting on the freeway. The majority of which were of the opinion that once again big business, whoever they were, had somehow interfered in the final decision. They wondered if some or all of the politicians had been bought. Things were really hotting up by the fourth program and the majority suggestion was that what was needed was a judicial enquiry. Once that was mentioned the campaign took up a far more serious position.

Now politicians and legal experts became involved and eventually the Governor himself was obliged to comment. Of course he had no objection to a judicial enquiry, since it would be in relation to a previous incumbent of the office of Governor, a Republican, and so, in a fit of moral outrage and indignation, he took ownership of it and guaranteed that it would be in place within six months. Something that both Don and Butch were determined to hold him to. They were on to a winner.

Chapter 40

By the time they got an appointment to interview Mark Reilly, the final member of The Wolf Pack, he was obviously well prepared for their questions. Like the others he lauded the enterprise of the group and emphasized how they had used local experts when they thought fit to do so. This Joey must surely have been one such expert but for the life of him, he could not remember anyone of that name assisting them. Of course he promised to reflect on it and assured them that he would be in contact if he recalled anything of note. However, unlike the others, he wanted assurances that he would be protected by the police and wasn't at all pleased to hear that his protection was, initially, his own responsibility.

On their way back to the station Eddie got a call from Dan Crosier to say that the State Police had spotted the Ford Taurus in the general area of Wayward Creek and had followed it to a house in the outskirts of the town. Whether the driver was Sean Stenson or not, they couldn't say. They wanted to know what they should do now.

"Hi Dan, just keep him under observation for the moment. In the meantime, you might see if you can find out where Stenson is staying. I will call you as soon as I get back to the station," said Eddie.

"I'm afraid our friend Sean Stenson has left the address we got for him," said Crosier when Eddie called him back. "He didn't leave a forwarding one. According to the landlord, mail is still being left for him and is being collected periodically."

"Damn it! Is this another blind alley? When are we going to get a break?" muttered Eddie. Then walking out to Maria's desk he said, "Sean Stenson, the guy with the Ford Taurus has left the address we got from registration. Will you do a search on him and see if we have any record of him in our system?"

"Have we what!" said Maria, an hour later. "Our friend Stenson has quite a record. In the past twenty years he has spent over fifty per cent of it as a guest in our prison system; armed robbery, assault with a deadly weapon, blackmail, just to mention a few of his charms."

Eddie immediately called Crosier back. "Dan, this guy Stenson needs to be closely watched. See if you can pull him in for possession of drugs or some traffic violation. My source up there tells me that it isn't cigarettes he smokes. See how he reacts."

When Eddie reported what he had discovered, the Chief said, "Ok, so he has quite a prison record for a man in his late forties, but that doesn't prove anything. What have we got? It appears that the car that is registered in his name was seen in the vicinity of Gregg Newman's house prior to the murder and that the same car was in the mall car park on the same day. So tell me where the crime is in any of these?" The Chief and Eddie were seated in the Chief's plush new office, into which he had moved two days earlier. Eddie and Lennie's units were due to move back the following weekend. "We can't arrest him or question him in relation to any of these."

"I agree totally," admitted Eddie, "but, I have asked our state colleagues to pick him up on a possible possession of drugs issue. Just to see what we can get out of him."

"Are you clutching at straws Eddie?"

"No, I really don't think so Chief. As I always say, there are no such things as coincidences, and I don't think that car showing up as it did, was in anyway a coincidence. So let us see what turns up over the next few days and if nothing does, then we cut him loose."

"OK, but you do realize that because Stenson is officially resident in Oakville according to the car registration, anything that our state colleagues do for us is a favor so to speak. I do however have a good relationship with Pete Colberg up in the Wayward Creek precinct; he was in the class just behind me. I will ask him to nose around and keep us posted."

Chapter 41

"Well did you find anything of interest in my file?" asked Joe Breslin. It was Friday evening and he and Eddie were sitting in the bar of the Colonial Hotel having a well-deserved after-work drink on the Friday.

"As a matter of fact that's something I need to talk to you about. Yes, it was of great help to us. The Ford Taurus that four of your witnesses thought they saw – well now we firmly believe that they did see it. We have independent information on such a car and are trying to trace it. The address of the registered owner is here in Oakville though the guy doesn't live at the address but seems to be using it as a convenient address. My question to you is, can we use your witness statements as they stand or do we now need to interview each one again? Have you any objection to either of those suggestions?"

"First of all, I must say I am delighted that the testimonies corroborate what you have now discovered. However, as I got those statements on the basis that they were in connection with the case we were defending, I would think that you will need to get fresh testimonies if you intend to use them in a different case. Leave it with me and I will check out with each of the witnesses and see if they are ok with that."

"Thanks, I appreciate that," said Eddie. "By the way, I hear that Newman is due for release in the next week or so. How did he survive the time inside?

"Yeah, he is coming out on Tuesday but it will be a very low-key release. Absolutely no media presence. I must say that the last time I saw him it shocked me to see how devastated he was. He was just a shadow of the man I defended less than a year ago. I honestly believe that if he hadn't turned state's witness and got a deal for early release in return, he would not have survived. Prison life is very unforgiving, especially for what is known as white collar criminals."

"Any idea where he will go and what he will do?" said Eddie as he finished off his beer.

"No idea, and if I did I couldn't tell you. Client confidentiality and all of that kind of stuff, you know. But why do you ask Eddie?"

"Maybe just idle curiosity or maybe I would like to ask him a few questions. I know that I can't. Let's leave it at that. Someday I will tell you what the questions would be. Now are you going to stand there with your hands in your pockets or are you going to get me a drink? In case you didn't notice, my glass is empty!"

Two hours later, having solved all of the world problems and replayed all the recent football matches, they decided it was time to head home.

Chapter 42

On Sunday night Eddie was surprised to get a call from Bradshaw to say that Alice had called him late on Friday night to say that she now recalled more about the guy she had named as Joey. She wondered if she could see Eddie on Monday morning at eleven a.m. as she would be in Oakville that morning. Apparently she remembered one of The Wolf Pack, saying something about the Governor's office urgently waiting for it, whatever 'it' was. And that if he didn't finish the report or something that sounded like report, it would cost the group millions and that they were not prepared to let that happen.

On Monday morning when Eddie got back to his own office after his usual meeting with the Chief he found a note to call Doctor Moody. Immediately he called him.

"Good morning Doctor. Sorry I missed your phone call. Hope you are keeping well?" said Eddie.

"Ah, Detective, thank you for getting back to me. It can get lonely here from time to time. No one seems to want my services any more. They tell me that the internet is now the new G.P... just go online and tell whoever is out there what your symptoms are and voilá you get a message back telling you what is wrong with you. Can you believe that, Detective? We are becoming obsolete, that's what is happening."

"Yes." said Eddie humoring him. "It must be tough living on your own with nothing to do. What keeps you going from day-to-day?"

"Well, I walk quite a lot when the weather allows. While I am walking I am snooping. And let me tell you Detective, it is amazing what I see. My eyes are still alive, I am glad to say."

"So tell me what you saw that interested you. I know you want to tell me. So enough suspense, spill the beans!"

"Don't spoil my pleasure, Detective, let me enjoy telling the story. Of late I have taken to walking past your friend Ms Starling's house and as I pass by, I take a little time to observe it. The first time I noticed it was early last week and then again on, I think it was Tuesday last that I noticed it again…"

"What did you notice?" interrupted Eddie.

"Patience my friend, patience please. Anyway as I was saying, since then I noticed it a few more times, a man! A man moving around the house. The first time I noticed him he was going in the front door. The next time he was getting into a car. It was only by walking past the house a few more times that I realized that it wasn't just a man, there were three different men coming and going around her house! Now what do you make of that?"

"Perhaps they were workmen," suggested Eddie. "As you previously mentioned, she was settling in to her new house so maybe she wanted alterations done. Is that a possibility Doctor?"

"No, these didn't look or act like workmen. As a matter of fact, I got the impression that they didn't want me to see their faces as I passed by. I bid one of them the time of day but he just turned away from me."

"Can you describe any of them for me?"

"Well, I would estimate that the guy getting into the car was in his mid to late forties. About five ten and as bald as a billiard ball, a tough looking character. The other two were also in their forties, one was very well dressed in a nice dark suit while the other, judging from the smell, seemed to be smoking grass every time I passed. He was probably not allowed smoke in the house, a kind of shifty guy. They all seemed to have keys to the house and were very much at home there. Maybe Starling was having a party!"

"You mentioned that you felt that doctors were becoming obsolete. Well if you keep up your observations, we, the police, will be obsolete Doctor! Thank you very much. This information is just what we are looking for. Tell me, would it be possible for you to get the make and registration number of the car? We would very much appreciate it if you could."

"That should be no problem." responded Moody.

Thirty minutes later Doctor Moody called Eddie with the car registration number of a Ford Taurus. Eddie immediately headed for the Chief's office.

"Please tell me that you have a breakthrough," was the Chief's welcome when he saw the excited look on Eddie's face.

"Maybe, just maybe," replied Eddie. "Apparently Ms Starling is keeping very strange company up in Wayward Creek. Our good friend Doctor Moody has advised us that she has three middle-aged men staying in her house, no crime there you may say. But one of them it would appear is none other than our friend Sean Stenson. His Ford Taurus is parked in the driveway and Doctor Moody described him exactly as his mug-shot does."

"Great work Eddie. That certainly changes the picture. I have already been on to Pete Colberg in State Police requesting a low-key surveillance for the car but in the light of what you tell me, I think we need to escalate that to a higher level. We need to find out who they are and what they are doing in Ms Starling's house. No more softly-softly!"

Just then Maria poked her head around the door to tell

Eddie that Bradshaw and Alice were waiting to see him. Excusing himself and promising the Chief that he would be back as soon as he finished taking a further statement from Alice he Joined Bradshaw and Alice who were seated in his office with Maria.

"Thanks for coming in again," began Eddie. "We very much appreciate all the assistance you have given us."

"No problem," said Bradshaw. "Alice is actually here with me to finalize the purchase of a lovely bungalow in Oldtown."

"That's very exciting for you." exclaimed Maria.

"It is indeed, hopefully it is the beginning of a new and a happy life for her." replied Bradshaw.

"I think every one of us hope that that will be the case." said Eddie.

"Now to get down to business," said Bradshaw. "It was while I was talking to Alice yesterday that she just remarked on the chat she had with you recently. She thought that what she had recalled might help."

"Yes," said Alice, who then went back over the recollections she had of the events that took place in her home, before continuing, "However, over the past few days I felt that there was something about the questions you were asking that were familiar. Later on I had a recollection that while I was a patient at the clinic, someone else had asked me the very same questions on more than one occasion. I wasn't sure, but I did not think that it was Doctor Mitchum who was asking them. Does that help in any way?"

"That's strange, who would want to know that?" replied Eddie. "It must fit somewhere in the jigsaw. Let me think on it and see if it makes sense and thanks for the information. If you have any other recalls, let me know."

Thanking them for their help and wishing Alice every happiness in her new home, he returned to the Chief's office and filled him in on what Alice had reported.

Chapter 43

The following day State Trooper, Pete Colberg who wasn't one to procrastinate, called the Chief with the news. That morning he had arranged for a state patrol car to be waiting for the Ford Taurus as it drove into the town, and pulled it over. According to his papers the drivers name was Sean Stenson with an address in Oakville. However, he said that he was staying locally with friends, just a social visit. The patrolman requested that he accompany him to the police station as the Oakville police were looking for the car in connection with a traffic violation. He was there in the station, awaiting questioning. "Would you prefer to have one of your guys to do the questioning or would you be happy for us to do it?" he asked.

Having thanked him for his help, the Chief explained that as their interest in the car and its driver was in connection with a multiplicity of serious offences, he would very much appreciate if his investigating officer, Detective Eddie McGrane, was given the opportunity to conduct the interview.

Within fifteen minutes Eddie and Maria were, once more, on their way north to Wayward Creek.

"Good morning Mr Stenson," said Eddie as they

entered the interview room two hours later. "My name is Detective McGrane and this is my partner Detective Diego. We are both stationed in Oakville, your home town."

"What has this got to do with Oakville? I was driving within the speed limits and there is nothing wrong with my car and I know nothing about a traffic violation. I want out of here now!" was Stenson's retort.

"All in good time," replied Eddie, "before you go, we need to ask you a few questions. The sooner you answer the sooner you go. Ok?"

"Questions about what?"

"Well, let's start with your address. What is your address?"

"My address is on my driving licence. Check it out yourself."

"Yes we have already checked it out but we were told that you don't reside at that address. So if you don't reside there, where do you reside Mr Stenson?"

"But that is my address. Naturally I don't always reside there. As far as I know there is no law that says I must, is there? When I am visiting friends in other parts of the state I stay with them."

"I see, so who are you staying with at this exact point in time?"

"Friends here in Wayward Creek, as you probably know."

"And do these friends have names?"

"I need a lawyer," replied Stenson.

"Certainly," said Eddie, "by all means if you feel you need one. However, before that we need to have you checked out for alcohol and drugs so that we have you formally processed. The patrolman who stopped you seemed to think that the butt-end you threw out the window wasn't a cigarette end, and being very litter conscious, not only had he recorded it on the car camera, but he was good enough to retrieve it. So, let me remind you that as you are on parole since your last visit to our state's prison system, any breach of that and you are back inside once more. Now I don't think you would want to go down that road again but if you still insist on getting your lawyer we will hold you until you organize for him to come."

Eddie stood up and began gathering his papers.

"Wait a minute." said Stenson, panic written all over his face. "What are you promising me?"

"I'm not promising you anything, mister." replied Eddie. "But if you co-operate with us, it just might make things easier for you. So let's start again. Where are you staying at the moment?"

"I'm staying with friends, the Ashtons," muttered a much more subdued Stenson.

"Tell me about them, the name is very familiar."

"I met Karl when we were both in prison some years ago. He watched my back a few times. I was out before him, so when he got out he contacted me. His sister and brother have a house up here. We meet up here from time to time."

Eddie looked at Maria and Maria looked at Eddie with her mouth half open in shock.

"What is his sister's name?" asked Eddie, while trying to keep a straight face.

"Jane, she works at the local Haven Clinic."

"Would that be Jane Starling?" asked Eddie.

"Yes, she was married to a soldier, Mo Starling, who never returned from Iraq and she still uses her married name."

"So you met Karl in prison. What was he in for?"

"The first time was because he decked a guy whom he thought was responsible for his father's death. For that he got a month in prison. A complete set up it was, but that's the way it works. These guys can rob and cheat and get away with it. The little guy hasn't a chance. The second time was for possession of drugs. Another set up for which he got twelve months."

"What was his father's name?" Eddie asked.

"Joey."

"Joey what?"

"Ashton"

"And who did he think was responsible for Joey's death?"

"I don't know." Stenson shook his head. "I think it was a bunch of no good bastards from Oakville. I really don't know."

"I think you know a lot more that you want to tell us, Stenson. But let me tell you that we know a lot more than you think. We have evidence that links you directly to an incident that took place at the home of Gregg Newman two years ago, an incident in which a young girl was killed. Yes, Mr Stenson we have a lot of questions to ask you in connection to that and depending on your cooperation or otherwise, you will be residing once more as a guest of the state."

"Look! I can only go on what I was told," began Stenson. "According to Karl, his father died by suicide. At first it was put down to pressure of work and the fact that he had produced a controversial report on a freeway project. However, sometime later Karl discovered a four-paged note that his father had written which explained why he had decided to end his life."

"Where did he find the note?" asked Maria.

"He found it after he was released from his first stay in prison. It was when he was clearing out the house before putting it on the market."

"So what did the note say?" asked Eddie.

Stenson then went on to say that according to the note Karl's father had been approached by Al McNally asking him to do a report which would suggest that the proposed freeway be diverted nearer to Oldtown. When he refused, McNally had threatened to reveal some indiscretion in his father's past.

"In other words he was blackmailing him," interjected Eddie.

"Yes," replied Stenson.

"So what did Karl do when he found the suicide note?"

"He went to the local police station and handed it in. That was the last he saw of it. The following day he was arrested for possession of drugs that were found in his car. A charge he strongly denied. They had been planted there. He had been set up."

Stenson stopped, drank some water from the glass on the table and proceeded with his story.

According to him, it was then that Karl and his brother, realizing that they couldn't depend on the police to do anything, decided to take the law into their own hands. With his help and their sister's input they set out to get revenge on those responsible. It was easy for them to identify who was responsible once they had McNally's name in the suicide note. Luckily Karl had the sense to keep a copy of it before handing it to the police. He wouldn't make the same mistake twice."

"So their first easy option was to upset the planned Mayoral Election." Stenson went on. "With the help of Jane, who knew exactly what Alice's movements were, they tried to put Gregg in a compromising situation. Unfortunately, that went wrong as the babysitter strangled as she fought against the belt they had put around her neck."

"So what part did you play in all of this?" asked Eddie.

"Look, I was only a driver," said a rattled Stenson. "It was all supposed to be a very simple set up. I did nothing wrong."

"But you have just admitted that you were part of the plan to get revenge on those who were responsible for Mr Ashton' death and that plan resulted in another death. You can't just walk away from that." said Maria.

"As I said, I was just a driver. I would get information on certain buildings and people's movements if they asked me. That's all. Sometimes I would drive them to the places they wanted to see. What they did afterwards was none of my business."

"I'm afraid it is not as easy as that," retorted Eddie,

"whether you like it or not, you are implicated in three murders; Angie Lummox, Leo Forrest and Jeff Suarez. Now think about it while we check up on a few things." said Eddie as Maria and he exited the room. As soon as they got outside Eddie called the Chief and filled him in on the interview.

"So what you are saying," said the Chief, with satisfaction "is that here we have the three siblings of a man who died by suicide and a convicted criminal who admits to being involved with them in getting revenge on the people they claim were responsible for his suicide. We now need to get all three of them in for questioning and get a warrant to search the house."

Immediately Eddie and Maria went to the clinic and requested that Jane accompany them to the local police station for questioning. It didn't take long for her to break down under questioning. According to her, it was her brothers who wanted revenge. Her role was only in giving them information on Alice's movements and in placing certain items in her room. Initially she was charged with conspiracy to commit a crime against Gregg Newman and was eventually released on bail.

While she was being questioned, the State Police arrested Max and Karl, and brought them to separate police stations for questioning. In their subsequent search of the house they found a collage of photographs of The Wolf Pack pinned to the kitchen wall. They also discovered a number of ski-masks and sets of black outfits and latex gloves from which they were able to get DNA samples; enough incriminating evidence to charge them both with the murders of Leo Forrest and Jeff Suarez. Stenson's evidence was sufficient to charge them with the involuntary manslaughter of Angie Lummox.

Two months later, all four were brought to court and convicted on all counts.

During the court case the defence team produced the copy of the suicide note and together with the confessions signed by both Stenson and Starling the extent of the conspiracy soon emerged. A group of individuals known collectively as The Pack had hatched a plan to make their fortune by coercing, Joseph Ashton into providing a false geological report on the proposed new freeway route. Their plan was, with the help of the bank chairman, to borrow extensively from the Farmers Bank. Two separate loans were to be drawn down. The first one was to be drawn down by a syndicate, code-named Castor. This one was for the purpose of a much publicized land purchase in Oldtown and also for the purpose of designing and building a state of the art Municipal Center for the town. A center which they had no intention of building in Oldtown once they got compensation for the change in the freeway route.

In the meantime, a second, much larger loan, drawn down by a syndicate code-named Pollux, was to be quietly drawn down for the purpose of buying up large tracts of land in Oakville, all drawn on the Farmers Bank with Teddy Moran's help. Then, once the report was published and with the help of a very senior politician in the Governor's office in their pocket. they would claim compensation for the loss of the Oldtown scheme and make their killing on developing Oakville. A win-win situation.

Six weeks after their father's funeral, Karl, his youngest son had attacked Ben Green, the Managing Director of the Farmers Bank, accusing him of murdering his father. He had mistaken him for Mr Moran; he was arrested and sentenced to one month in prison on a charge of assault plus of having a quantity of drugs in his car. This second charge he hotly denied, claiming that the drugs had been planted there.

At the end of a six-week trial Karl and his brother Max Ashton together with Sean Stenson were found guilty of murder and attempted murder and sentenced to life imprisonment. Jane Ashton was sentenced to seven years for her part in the conspiracy.

McNally, Moran and Reilly were all subpoenaed to

appear before the Tribunal of Enquiry the Governor had set up to investigate the circumstances surrounding the rerouting of the freeway.

As for Alice, well, having purchased her new home in Oldtown, she set about rebuilding her life by going back to college to complete her law studies and starting a new life for herself and Tracey.

Chapter 44

Three months after the trial, Eddie and Shirley visited Alice in her new home in Oldtown. They were pleasantly surprised to see how well she had recovered from her ordeal. According to Alice, Tracey, who was out with friends had also settled in very quickly and was very happy in her new home and surroundings.

Once Alice had shown them around her new home and they were seated in the sitting room overlooking a well-kept garden, she wanted to know all the news from Oakville. In particular she wanted to know how the wedding plans were progressing.

"Well, Shirley and her Mom are in full flight." said Eddie. "I never realized how much planning went in to just saying 'I do'. Every shop in Oakville must have been visited in the last two months. What they are buying, I don't know!"

"Don't mind him Alice," responded Shirley with a grin. "He is just as wrapped up in the plans as I am. He just says that in front of his buddies just to sound macho. Anyway, now that you have brought up the subject, we have a favor to ask you. And don't be afraid to say no. Will you be our Matron of Honor, Alice? We would really love if you would. Remember it is only because of you that we met."

"Oh my God!" exclaimed Alice. "What an honor! Of course I would love to be part of such a special day! Thank you both so much!" she said as she jumped up and hugged each of them in turn, with tears in her eyes.

When they finally stopped talking about the details of the wedding and they had finished a beautiful meal that Alice had prepared for them, Alice asked Eddie if she could ask him some questions about the court case. There were so many aspects of the case that she couldn't come to grips with.

"Well now that the court case is over," said Eddie. "I suppose I am at liberty to answer some, if not all of your questions."

"Ever since the case ended I have been trying to put the pieces together but I just can't understand how it all developed," Alice went on. "Perhaps you can fill in the gaps for me."

"I certainly will, if I can," replied Eddie.

"Thanks. I would appreciate that."

"I think it all started, when the Ashton brothers realized that their father's death was the result of his dealings with The Wolf Pack," began Eddie. "Their initial and I suppose simply immediate reaction, was to assault one of those responsible. However, this resulted in Karl being convicted and sent to prison, which in turn infuriated the brothers further. They then reacted by planning to sabotage the upcoming Mayoral Election by discrediting their candidate, Gregg."

"So that's where Gregg came in!" said Alice.

"Yes, but that plan went wrong on two counts," continued Eddie. "Firstly you turned up at the house one day before Angie's death, when they were setting up the scene. They were convinced that you had spotted at least one of them and what they were doing. So they perceived you to be a threat. Secondly Angie died when she fought against the belt around her neck. It was never intended that she would die."

"So in reality, her death was an accident." said Alice.

"Yes exactly. However, in the meantime, fearing that you could identify them, they planned to kill you by interfering with the power steering in Doctor Mitchum's car, knowing that you would be driving it on that day. Remember, Jane Starling was their eyes and ears at the clinic. However, it was your good friend Doctor Mitchum who died," explained Eddie.

"But I don't ever remember seeing any one in the house on any of my visits," said Alice.

"But they weren't to know that! They assumed you

must have been aware of them in the house. They felt they had to silence you," continued Eddie.

"Oh my God!" exclaimed Alice. "I was that near to dying! And to think I trusted Jane Starling!"

"After that things got out of hand, with many a row between the brothers and their sister as to what to do next," Eddie went on. "During questioning it emerged that Karl had drawn up a plan to kill all of The Wolf Pack members and was responsible, on his own, for the killing of Jeff Suarez. Having, apparently got away with that they felt encouraged to go ahead and kill Leo Forrest as well."

"Luckily the killings ended there," said Shirley.

"So what will happen to the rest of The Wolf Pack?" asked Alice.

"Well," said Eddie, "as you well know, Tribunals of Enquiry move slowly and now doubt this one will be no different. However, I have great faith in our press and TV media. They won't let it slip away. I have feeling The Wolf Pack's troubles are not over yet!"

Made in the USA
Charleston, SC
18 October 2016